The Reluctant Spy

A geo-political thriller in the style of John Le Carré.

High praise for
fans of
geopolitical thrillers

"My grandfather actually-owned an orange farm in Israel. **The Reluctant Spy** is the best book I've read since "Cry, The Beloved Country."

Two men, born to be enemies. Over the course of their lives, their paths cross repeatedly -- sometimes by intention, sometimes by chance. Sometimes because of interference -- by whom? Muslim terrorists? the CIA? the Israeli Mossad?

The born enemies seem destined to meet again in the end -- but will they? If so, where? and when? and if so, how violent will things become? The author keeps you guessing. It's fun to see how it ultimately unfolds. A good read.

The characters embody the painful dualities, moral ambiguities, and human consequences behind the headlines. The story's blend of cultural insight, psychological nuance, and high stakes geopolitical tension creates a narrative that resonates powerfully with readers who appreciate serious, conflict centered fiction.

By the same author:

The President's Assassin

R.S.V.P.

Murder at Pebble Beach

The Reluctant Spy

A geo-political thriller in the style of John Le Carré.

Karen Hagestad Cacy

Portal Publications

Copyright © 2026 by Portal Publications

ISBN:

Print: 979-8-9944200-0-3

eBook: 979-8-9944200-1-0

Version: 1/4/2026 V2

Formerly published as *Return to Ismailia*

The Reluctant Spy

A geo-political thriller in the style of John Le Carré.

> "Where should we go after the last frontiers,
> where should the birds fly after the last sky?"
> Mahmoud Darwish

Achille Lauro Hijacking

Mediterranean Sea, October 1985

Four heavily armed Palestinian terrorists hijack the Italian cruise ship Achille Lauro, carrying more than 400 passengers and crew off Egypt. The hijackers demand that Israel free 50 Palestinian prisoners. The terrorists kill a disabled American tourist, 69-year-old Leon Klinghofer and throw his body overboard with his wheelchair.

1

Many years earlier in Old Palestine

The Levy family of Portland, Oregon finally fulfilled their dream of returning to their "homeland" in Israel. A devout family, each member – mother, father, brother and sister -- already had faithfully spent several summers here working in kibbutzim, helping to build the country they now called their own.

The family sold their home in the upscale Dunthorpe neighborhood of Portland, stretching their real estate substantially farther in this gated community shaded by a grove of olive trees. The Mediterranean blue sky, the Israeli air defense jets overhead, and the melting pot of Jews from around the globe, together served as daily reminders to Flo and Harold Levy of the major change they had seemingly so cavalierly made.

Their new three-bedroom home with its own courtyard and swimming pool went a long way to assuaging these immigrants' fears and newcomer uncertainties. Designed by a Portland architect in keeping with the development's specifications, the home was perfect in every way. Flo Levy had but to show her gardening acumen, Harold had but to position his favorite reading chair in the den, and the children, now adults, had but to schedule their frequent visits from their New York City base, where important jobs still held them.

Harold kept to his stateside schedule, regardless of his retirement from the bench. Up early, walk the dog to the corner bakery for hot rolls, a hot coffee for the short walk to the news stand, and then home. Judge Levy was an observant fellow, having spent most of his lifetime listening to the criminal, the downtrodden, and the just plain ridiculous, explain why they were before him in a court of law. His cataract-ridden eyes beneath bushy gray brows still scanned the horizon, still picked up nuances of body language, still held the intelligence and alertness of the American eagle.

During the first week of his Israeli morning regimen, he passed at precisely the same time each day, a young Palestinian youth, of around the age of twelve. The boy was clean and well-mannered in his light cotton gallabiyah robe and sandals. Each day, the guard at the gate would usher him through into the development. Judge Levy watched the routine steadily for five days running. The boy would make his way to a grove of orange trees located in the turnaround of his cul-de-sac. He would circumnavigate the grove three times with slow, reverential steps, talking to himself. Then the boy would sit cross-legged underneath a tree and slowly eat a fresh orange he had picked. Once finished, he would carefully round up all orange peelings, stuffing them into his pockets. He would then retrace his route, nodding at the development's sentry on his way out. The sentry always said the same thing: "Shalom." To which the boy's response also was the same: "Bis millah-hee."

Following five days of this routine, the Judge approached the sentry. Obviously, the lad was Palestinian. Obviously, the lad had no clear business in their guarded development. Obviously, his "orange regimen" seemed peculiar.

"Fouad Al-Najimi," he was told. That was the boy's name. "Son of Mustafa Al-Najimi, a formerly wealthy and powerful landowner in the area. Grower and exporter of oranges throughout Europe." "One day," the guard continued, "following the nationalization of the farmer's land to Israel, --- well, of course, we all made sacrifices for the new nation, --- it was decided to build homes. Well, listen, oranges, we had plenty of elsewhere in the country. It is told the boy, who was then only eight years of age, held his grandfather's hand as the two watched giant bulldozers clear away the last remnants of his orange grove to make way for the new development."

"He was compensated, of course," the Judge asked.

"Oh, sure, sure. All who lost land were compensated. His family was given a certain level of assurance, Israel's certificate of appreciation for services rendered the State. Actually, the old man and his family until today live in a tent city five miles down the road. Of course, his brothers are holding up his family's exit from that area. Arab politics!"

The man shrugged his shoulders in the universal symbol of resignation. Denoting, of course, with one motion, the intransigence of Arab authority, the complexities of land transferal, and the absolute hopelessness of it all.

The Judge continued: "And the boy?"

Again, the sentry shrugged. "Boys are boys n'est-ce pas? Loyal. Stands by his grand- father. Wouldn't you want your son or grandson to do the same? It is admirable. He is harmless. So, I bend the rules a bit, allow him his time to sit in what to him still is his grandfather's orange grove. We lose an orange a day from this activity. Who's to complain? What can it hurt?"

For the first time, Judge Levy felt the first impact of his decision in Portland, Oregon to join the fight for homeland here so far away. The clichés of Arab nationalism, of Arab claims to the land, of the immaturity of the Arab argument, suddenly developed some meat on their bones. For the first time, Judge Levy saw the struggle for what it really was – a fight for the land. Forget ideology for once. This was man against man, land parcel against land parcel. Rules – his rules, against someone else's rules. Winner against loser. In Judge Levy's clear analytic way, he had just made a sea change in his ideology. A sea change he would not soon share with anyone. A sea change of which he was more than ashamed.

For now, his musings would remain where they belonged, in the private recesses of his professorial mind. Too much conflict to bring them out into the open. Too much confusion. Too much politics. For an old man, who had made the right decision for his family. For at this time of his life, he would not make another stand. Would not take up the cudgel. Would not go against his own. They were, in his last years on earth, all he had. Family. Religion. Country.

The Judge walked slowly home, his downcast eyes focused on the hard, sunbaked Israeli earth passing beneath his feet.

2

"The master-key of opinion lay in the common language: where also lay the key of imagination. Their heritage of the Koran and classical literature held the Arab-speaking peoples together. Patriotism, ordinarily of soil or race, was warped to a language."
T.E Lawrence, "Seven Pillars of Wisdom"

Fouad al Najimi was a child of Palestine. That made him part of "the Palestine situation." Polite words for a world's decision – to recompense one damaged civilization with the belongings of another. For those Palestinians so 'inconvenienced,' there was a variety of responses, coping mechanisms, life decisions.

Tough men fought for the land, meeting settlers in armed combat. The wealthy bought their way out. Ma'aleesh. Face facts. Move on. The weak were neutralized through illness and death. The obstinate took up positions of absentee ownership, grasping their land deeds in tent cities many miles away from their former homes. With only their memories, these people refused to move lest their refugee status be erased, and with it, their land claims as well.

To the casual observer, Fouad's grandfather, the orange grower, was just another farmer holding yellowed land deeds secreted in a dusty cookie tin. But the elder Al Najimi was unique among the displaced. Al Najimi was a man obsessed with the long view. Seeing into the future, the man jumped over the present, ignoring it as one would an unwrapped gift. He could predict the modern intransigence of the camps. He might even have predicted the emergence of the Intifada and international terrorism.

He was a man who saw more than others. He was one who sat alone thinking. While others took action or fell into despair, Al Najimi took his solace in language and literature, not bullets. For a farmer to turn the other cheek and take up the literary life huddled in a hot, dirty refugee tent was unbelievable.

Others in the family thought the old man had lost his marbles. Reading, rocking to and fro, then writing essay after essay after essay. Different people take their rage in different ways. The old man turned his anger inward. To the written word. Because he believed the Jew would win in the end. Beyond man's end, however, he believed would be the judgment. The scrolls. The archives. And it was for that end that the old man worked. He was the watcher. Not the warrior. Watcher's words would last. Warrior's acts would disappear in the sands of the desert.

It was this role model that was presented to Fouad, "Fou-Fou," the grandson. Learning. Accommodation through knowledge. The historical long view. Moderation. Clean living. Clean thinking. Fou-Fou was imprinted by aristocratic values, even as he tasted the daily grit of sand in his evening meal. And as desert winds blew open the tent flap, Fou-Fou's grandfather's hand on his shoulder steadied the youngster. There were the daily lessons. In Arabic. In desert literature. But, cannily, the old man also passed along French and English, history of the West, math and science. He would prepare the grandson for his own future, not the hereafter.

Curiously, amid the crushing poverty of the refugee camp, the old man had long ago learned to "Trust in God, but tie the camels." A frugal man his entire life, the man had resources stashed in several special locations – places of impeccable safety known only to him. It was this attention to resources that allowed the man to break his precious grandson from the poor confines of the camp.

Fou-Fou, with his precise British English inflection, finally was deposited, fully paid, onto the doorstep of a British private school in the mountains of Lebanon. Arrangements were made for the boy's passport and papers – nothing a little baksheesh couldn't fix. And so it happened that Fou-Fou, from the age of 14 was entrusted to foreigners for the balance of an estimable education.

Westerners were schooled in Arabic at this mountain village school. Spies were prepared for the British Empire and later, the American Empire. For the school to accept a young Palestinian in their midst was quite untoward. But the generous donation by the grandfather, combined with the intriguing notion of having a future "enemy" in their midst worked in Fou-Fou's favor.

Here, the young man was schooled in French,

German and even Hebrew – an unheard- of mix of languages for the normal young Palestinian youth. In addition, he lettered in soccer, and became an excellent tennis player. Polo was denied him – there were limits even to his grandfather's wealth. But the fulsome education of a young British international gentleman was not denied him. The handsome young man learned to dance, to discern fine wines, and which fork to use first. He was trained in respectfulness for his elders, compassion for the down-trodden, and confidence in his own abilities.

Several times a year, Fou-Fou was returned to the camps, to visit his aging grandfather. It was in the camps that he developed a silent, but gnawing, cultural schizophrenia. At school, he could adopt the irony of the upper- class Brit. In the camps, he became the street fighter, intent on killing Jews. With his grandfather, he was the young respectful scholar. When his pals accused him of putting on airs, of becoming westernized, it was his grandfather's wise counsel that taught the young man how to keep a foot balanced in each culture.

Thus, it came to pass that Fou-Fou was an Arab chameleon. Adept in both worlds. Confused as to his place in each world. Astride a horse of two colors, racing in opposite directions simultaneously. Understanding each side as an insider. And hating each side's foibles. Fou-Fou's hatreds were of the hardened steel one finds in families. The more one knows, the more hateful one can potentially become. Going for the soft underbelly. Hitting below the belt. Taking inside knowledge to malevolent ends. Because when one knows both sides, one can become either side. Mahleshe. What does it matter which side? So long as life is good. What good is revenge when there are pretty women, fine wines, and the aroma of power?

Upon graduation, Fou-Fou made his way back to his grandfather. He was several days too late. The old man had passed away in his sleep, with the grit of desert sands clenched between his teeth. He died a happy man content in the knowledge of his grandson's entry into the world. He knew that great things would come of such a man. A man schooled in the desert and in the drawing-room . A man who had roots everywhere. A man from whom much would be asked. A man who, one day, would find himself, his true meaning, his destiny and that of his elders. A man, finally, of Palestine.

3

"All your friends are false; all your enemies are real."
Mexican proverb

Many years later . . .

It was 11:15 a.m. in downtown Cairo, and the heat was beginning to roil upwards from the city streets, mixing with car exhaust and the aromas of 47-11 cologne (a favorite of Arab men), and coffee. Cairo's busy, crowded streets resembled those in most third world countries – horns honking, men yelling in foreign dialects, wind-driven candy wrappers slamming into the curb, the sound of donkey bells as wagons over-filled with wares made their way among the stalled taxicabs.

Kenneth L. Rossberg, "Rossie" to his friends, rushed on foot down Sharia Kasr El Aini, late for his appointment with the "Second Undersecretary in Charge of Everything but Critical Thinking" at a hidden away mid-town satellite office of the U.S. Embassy. At the ripe old age of fifty, the former professor had been pressed into service – a Jew fluent in Arabic – against the next big terrorist believed to be operating here, now, somewhere in Egypt.

He arrived in Cairo several weeks earlier – long enough to contract "gyppie tummy," the notorious 'Egyptian tummy,' that visitors contract from Cairene germs transmitted in watermelon, lettuce, and water. Even an inadvertent splash of Nile River water can deliver the germ. It is a morbidly effective form of weight control. Rossie's weight fluctuated 30 to 40 pounds based on his trips to Egypt. He was sure that at some point his aging body would implode, but so far, it seemed to be a mere matter of getting to a bathroom in time, before he had an unfortunate accident. Exotic travel. Nothing like it, he thought to himself this day, as he searched for relief.

A voice nearby whispered to him, "Over here, habibi." What the devil? He turned to face a woman in black robes, but a woman with a man's voice. "Come with me. Sayid Rossberg, isn't it?"

"Ma'aleesh. Thanks anyway. I appreciate your

concern," Ken muttered in street Arabic. Suddenly, he found himself surrounded by a group of "women," all in the traditional dress. But the faces were not soft and feminine with black-rimmed kohl eyes. These eyes, and the voices that accompanied them, were sinister and masculine. With a single wave of black robes moving along the dusty sidewalk, the group of eight or ten silently and efficiently moved him off the crowded street and into an alley and roughly threw him into the back of a waiting taxi.

Who in downtown Cairo at midday would question a bunch of silly women moving as a flock of scared geese? Isn't that how women should behave? Heads bowed. Residing in the shadows. When outdoors, always in a chaste group of their kind, so no mistakes might be made, no assignations kept, no notice taken. The Egyptian woman must at all times be beyond suspicion. And so, what better masquerade for men wishing to hide themselves and an unseemly mission than dressed as women.

Rossie had been a desk jockey back home in Washington. His academic life spent translating dust-covered Arabic tomes appealed to him. Happiness consisted of sitting in his favorite easy chair, with a good reading lamp, peace and quiet. His wife, Rachel, also a professor of Islamic studies, shared his penchant for a sedentary lifestyle. Together, they had settled on a serene, albeit un-ambitious existence for themselves in a small cottage located at Scientists Cliffs, Maryland overlooking the Chesapeake Bay.

At night, surrounded by stacks of books, research papers, dual computers and reading lamps, the two would spin their intellectual fantasies accompanied by the soothing strains of Mozart. Rossie would occasionally look up from his work to notice a large ship passing through the channel below. Most pleasure craft knew enough to stay off the Bay at night due to the twin terrors of Naval Intelligence testing who-knew-what, and the sudden squalls that rendered this narrow part of the Bay particularly lethal to other than large ships.

As time went by, life enveloped the two in their shared goals of raising their only son, Kenneth Jr., amid a stable scholarly environment. Books were stacked everywhere. Many had page markers reminding the reader of a nugget to be interpolated with other nuggets in search of arcane conclusions, shared by a handful of other scholars, or, eventually, a sharp researcher in the Near Eastern section at the U.S. State Department.

In the past six months the international war on terror had hit close to home, propelling Rossie against his own wishes into a new life of travel and clandestine meetings often accompanied by a constant gnawing terror where his stomach used to be. As a spy, he was a near-total failure. His only claim to fame, the reason for being in these hell-holes, was his proficiency in the Arabic language. For a Jew to know English, Hebrew and Arabic was rare in this culture clash of a world-gone-mad.

It was his first visit to Washington's Freer Gallery of Art, where his lifelong obsession with Arabic calligraphy had begun. For it was art that hooked him in the beginning, not some world-weary strategy for full employment in his late forties. The beauty of the timeless classical Arabic transfixed him. As he studied, he realized the depth and poetry of this ancient language. Such high-mindedness escaped his handlers back at Langley however. What they cared about were results. Never mind the nomadic poet wandering in the desert fantasy. For the Company's warriors, it was his Arabic and Hebrew fluencies, plus a certain Sephardic darkness of skin which allowed him to "pass" as an Arab, that brought him to their attention.

In any event, wasn't "the Jew" under the skin but a genetic brother of "the Arab?" In espionage, the era of "human intelligence" had returned. There was no computer program, it turned out, which could replicate secrets whispered to friends in the dark alleys, coffee houses and souks of the Middle East. And so, his government had enrolled him to impersonate his 'brother' – to travel the back streets of the world, carrying a pistol he barely could shoot. For assignations. And information. Always information.

Now, someone was throwing a damp, smelly cloth over his head and tying it around his throat. Kenneth Rossberg felt himself wedged between two of the men in the back. No sooner was he seated than his lower muscles gave way. The all-too familiar liquid began running down his pant-leg and onto the cab floor. The unwelcome odor mixed with the smell of his captors' sweat and his own terror. Who were these men? How did they know his name? And why, in the name of God, were they speaking with Palestinian accents?

Ken Rossberg, Agent #038-AH according to a dossier located in a file cabinet back in Langley, knew very little. One thing was clear, however. His day was about to get a whole lot worse.

20

4

" . . . a Jew who wants to make a career working in or studying about the Middle East will always be a lonely man: he will never be fully accepted or trusted by the Arabs, and he will never be fully accepted or trusted by the Jews."

Thomas L. Friedman

Rossie could tell from a sudden upsurge in cacophony that the car had entered Cairo's busy Midan al-Tahrir ("Liberation Square.") traffic circle. "Funduq Hilton," by the Nile River fronted on the square. Tourists of all shapes and sizes spewed forth from the hotel's homogenized but protective façade. The Brits and Germans shared a discernible sturdiness, in their desert khaki shorts, cameras and sensible walking shoes. The French were more stylish and usually were smoking. Africans on holiday or on official government business often wore tribal, ceremonial garb – long flowing cotton robes of bright design. Americans looked, well,

American. The body language and self-absorption gave them away. Red Chinese and Arabs from other nations made up the rest.

Beyond the tall, faceless international hotel, settled on an urban island in the middle of the Nile River with its graceful felucca sailboats, was a remnant of the old British Empire – "Nadi Gezira," The Island Club. Here at the club on any given day, away from the bustle of one of the world's largest and most heavily populated and polluted cities, one could calmly sip one's "G and T" beside the smaller of two pools that bracketed the club's well-used polo field. Visitors remarked on the sight of the beautiful Egyptian women, with their slanted eyes, straight noses, and thick black hair – the results of years of marrying exclusively their own kind.

So pure was Cairo's upper-class gene pool, that one might consider substituting one's de rigueur visit to the Egyptian Museum by choosing instead to lift one's glass in comfort under a cabana at Nadi Gezira the better to view modern day Nefertiti's, who were themselves enjoying a sip and a smoke at the British bastion.

Head covers? Fundamentalist-imposed feminine

modesty? Not at Nadi Gezira. At this exclusive
encampment, the liquor flowed freely, faces were by Max
Factor, accents were distinctly British, and the subjects
ranged from ski vacations spent in Gstaad, to the latest
Paris couturier shows. Politics somehow failed to touch
this privileged class, who by accident of birth happened to
reside in the midst of an international 'danger zone.' The
reliable shields of money and class, as always, kept the
wolves at bay. Poolside, on any given day, one could
overhear besides Arabic, English, French, Italian or
German. Never, as Rossie could recall Swahili, despite
Cairo's preeminence in North Africa.

As his kidnap car became predictably stalled in
traffic, Rossie comforted himself with the knowledge that
they were still in a good part of town. With the luxurious
embassy district, "Garden City," feeding onto the square,
surely someone -- an American? -- in the midday crush
would notice a man with a bag over his head. He heard a
donkey braying just outside the rolled down window. He
could imagine the scene repeated countless times in this
busy traffic circle: the donkey's owner was tugging on a
rope around the donkey's neck as the stubborn animal
refused to proceed a step further with his heavy load.
Traffic, of course, would back up across the square as this

daily war of wills played out.

Today, as usual, the hapless traffic cop blew his whistle to no avail. Finally, noticing their car, he approached. Rossie felt a brief sense of relief and sat up straight the better to yell out. His scream was stifled however by the unmistakable butt of a revolver his seatmate had rammed under his shirt – the cold metal of the gun resting not so reassuringly against his bare skin. Rossie had a sense of despair mixed with terror as he noted the coolness of the metal against him on this hot day.

The cop addressed the driver, inquiring about his curious cargo in the back seat. Laughing, the driver recounted a colorful and plausible story about his soon-to-be brother-in-law, whom they had just trapped, kidnapped from work and were taking to his bachelor party set to last well into the evening and following day. The description, Rossie had to admit, was colorfully imaginative, filled with a healthy dose of sexual innuendo for the cop's benefit.

"Even as we are trapped in traffic, twenty of the finest dancers await the captured groom," his driver recounted. "Habibi will never be the same once we've done with him," he added to an appreciative audience. For the traffic cop, it was a welcome break in a hot, thankless day of guiding too many recalcitrant motorists around too small a space. As Rossie squirmed in his seat, the renewed pressure of metal on skin reminded him of his own powerlessness: "Play along, Jew," he was warned.

In due time, traffic cleared, and they were once again underway. Where were they taking him? As the car emerged from the traffic circle, Rossie noted a sudden peacefulness just outside the car windows. The hum of birds and the feel of cool summer shade signaled their entrance into Garden City. Most of Cairo could in fact be identified by aggravating noise pollution. Cars, masses of humanity, horns, donkeys braying, all provided an unrelenting backdrop of white noise in the city. Within the city limits, besides Nadi Gezira, only two neighborhoods knew peaceful quiet – Ma'adi, an exclusive residential area, and Garden City, home of the international community.

Abruptly, after only a few minutes' drive, the car turned into a drive and stopped at what he surmised was a guard house. Rossie knew they had not traveled far enough to be in Ma'adi. Even blindfolded, he could discern nearly to the block their location in Garden City. He lived in Garden City, reported to work at the Embassy here, and nodded each day to a number of sentries at foreign embassy entrances located along his pleasant tree-lined walking route. A guard house was not in and of itself a defining landmark in this part of town. Nor were old vine-covered mansions, guarded by armed guards, watch dogs, sentry towers, and entrances located behind sturdy cement anti-terrorism Jersey barriers.

"Iftah Yah Sim-Sim, ('Open Sesame')," yelled the driver.

A man outside responded with the greeting "Allahu Akbar." "God is Great."

Rossie heard the clank of a heavy gate being electronically opened. He was relieved to know that he was still in relatively familiar surroundings. Perhaps his captors' business with him would be brief and humane. Even as he had the thought, he knew the odds were stacked against it. This was planned, orchestrated. They knew his name. Friends at an estate, possibly even at an embassy, had been complicit in his taking. Who knew of this? Who were they answering to? What did they think he knew? What more did they know? Suddenly, he felt a chill. There was his family to consider. Had this "job" taken him and them too far already? Was any of this personal? Or was he so new, so raw a recruit to "the cause" that he was not yet privy to the mess he had stepped into?

How much of this related to his new "business," of which, truth be told, he to date knew far too little. It was his handlers who made sense of what he learned, not him. He was but "the listener." The buck stopped "there," in Langley, not "here," with Kenneth Rossberg, Sr. Of that the Company had assured him. He was but a cog in the West's vast intelligence network: "Forewarned is cheating," was their motto. And he was but one of many in an army positioned at keyholes. Nothing more, nothing less. Simple so far. Until today.

From behind his mask, Rossie enjoyed a brief moment of levity as he imagined his captors' surprise to learn what a dead fish they had on their hands. Could they really imagine him to be of use? Rossie was of medium height and build, with rapidly thinning gray hair. His legs turned slightly inward as he ambled along (he had never truly perfected homo sapiens' walk), head cast downward, thoughts inward. He had never shaken his age-old self-consciousness and lack of confidence. In fact, he fairly reeked of these less than manly qualities. No. Clearly, these fellas had the wrong man. Wrong for them, but of more immediate import to Rossie, wrong for him.

5

Rossie was man-handled and shoved out of the car, a feat most uncomfortable given that he still had the cloth tied firmly about his head. He was roughly led up several outside steps and from what he could imagine, directly into the front of a large building, either an embassy, large private home or other semi-official structure. He noted two things straight away as he was seated on a large, comfortable sofa – a strong, womanly jasmine cologne scent, and the rattle of a distant and failing air conditioner.

"Imshi!" A male voice close at hand ordered, and the rustle of a woman's skirts passed very near him, trailing the sweet familiar Egyptian scent as she obeyed the command and left the room. The voice of the leader then ordered the men to prepare themselves. A moment later, someone yanked the covering from Rossie's head. He looked up, blinking at the bright sunshine filtering into the room through tall windows onto priceless antiques and

Oriental rugs. As the room came into focus, Rossie could see that his captors had temporarily reversed roles with Rossie, as they now all wore short black hoods, their eyes glinting in his direction.

The surreal nature of black-hooded terrorists with victim in an elegant drawing room was abruptly broken by the commander's harsh expletives. Perhaps, something had gone wrong. Perhaps they were expecting someone else. They had captured the wrong man. "Of course, that was it," Rossie thought. He was too small a fish to net. He could have told them that straight away, saved them all the trouble.

His day was quickly turning from a B-drama into a B-comedy. A string of swear words in both French and Arabic ensued.

"Merde alors," said one man. "Just look at him. Did you even look at him in the street?" Hands waved, fingers pointed in his direction. Hell, he could as easily have gotten to his feet and walked out then and there, all the attention he was getting. As he briefly considered it, he noticed a menacing presence just at the hallway entry, a swarthy fellow equipped with what appeared to be a long hunting knife. On second thought . . .

One man standing behind him kept fingering Rossie's thinning gray hair. Another repeatedly jabbed the butt of his rifle into Rossie's stomach. Then the men began to see the humor in their mistake.

"What was the man thinking?"

"Could this be the demon spawn?" This comment was met by raucous laughter.

"Hell, maybe we should just take this guy out. Just look at him."

Another man: "Every family tree has one of these. Most are hardly noticed. Except by you men. Nice work. Now what are we to do?"

"Throw the fish back. We've done our job. This was to send a message. We've done our jobs now."

The bag was quickly retied around Rossie's neck. The woman was called. "Noor!" "Here. Take him." At this the woman reached down for his hand. She led him down a long hallway and then down two flights of stairs. When they reached the landing, she removed his head covering, having adjusted her own so he could not recognize her features. Her left hand still held onto his, like a schoolgirl with her first boyfriend. The right hand, however, held a revolver that was trained on him.

"Imshi!" she ordered in a soft voice.

They proceeded down a succession of underground passages. A number of wooden doors marked the hallway. At one of those doors, the woman paused. She removed a fresh orange from a pocket that was hidden in her flowing skirt and handed it to Rossie. Then she unlatched the door, and abruptly shoved Rossie out onto a busy downtown street.

"Yallah!" ("Hurry!") As his eyes adjusted to the bright light, the door was quickly shut and re-latched behind him. Rossie was a free man, standing once more in city traffic, curiously holding an orange.

He had been gone, he could surmise, nearly two hours. Long enough to have missed his meeting at the Embassy satellite office. Such was his relationship with his new handlers that Rossie actually considered thinking of a more mundane excuse than that he had just been taken by kidnapers off a downtown street at midday. Taken and released?! Who would believe him? Taken and held, yes. Taken and decapitated, of course. Taken for ransom and his body found floating in the Nile River, certainly. But taken and released? Like some underweight trout caught from a mountain stream? More likely, he had taken hashish with lunch and had himself an unscheduled nap. Now that, for a man such as Rossie, was far more believable.

Rossie decided he had had enough for one day. For one thing, he needed a shower to clean up followed by a long, soaking bath to unwind. One would think he also needed to think. For some strange reason, however, his inclination was to put the event from his mind. He was here. He was alive. 'Next-of-kin' hadn't been contacted. No one was worried. All he really had to contend with would be one mad-as-hell boss. And after the day he had had, he was in no mood for angry bosses just now. And so, as the muezzins climbed up to their minarets for the late afternoon call to prayer, Rossie made his own way, back to his pension in Garden City, this time above ground.

He made his way to his cool, tiled bathroom, turning on the fan. A cold beer accompanied his lukewarm bath. He lay back in the tub, letting the drink cool and calm him. He thought of his son back in the States. In due course, he concocted a lie. He decided that he needed to be at home due to a 'family situation.' He decided to take a break, possibly permanent, from this so-called spy work on his own terms. If Langley didn't like it, they could shove it right up their stupid asses. Such was Kenneth Rossberg's state of mind on this atypical day of duty in the Egyptian wilderness.

Eventually, he peeled and ate the orange, the only tangible souvenir of what had transpired.

That gentle calligraphy could have brought Rossie to this day, to these events, and to this new darker turn of mind, was not foreseen. Rossie felt himself turning a corner in his life. He vowed to take more care of himself, to obey fewer orders. To set new boundaries for himself. The scholar becoming "action man." Well, not exactly. Perhaps the scholar becoming "more a man of action." "That will do, Rossie," he thought. "That will do."

6

"Oh, what is the matter with poor Puggy-wug? Pet him and kiss him and give him a hug. Run and fetch him a suitable drug. Wrap him up tenderly all in a rug. That is the way to cure Puggy-wug."
Winston Churchill

Rossie awoke with a bad headache, but unlike the majority of foreigners taken hostage in the Middle East, otherwise none the worse for wear. Before he left the bed, he went over the events of the previous day. Had he been dreaming? Noticing his soiled trousers crumpled in a corner, he knew he had not been. But at the same time, he instinctively knew, as he had the day before, that under no circumstances should he tell anyone about the incident. It was, after all over. Chal'as. Done with.

Place it on the detritus scrap heap of his life and move on. This resolve remained with him while dressing, and as the servant poured him his first strong cup of

Egyptian coffee. It stayed with him as he ate his eggs and potatoes, cooked American style. As he exited his apartment onto the pleasant tree-lined avenue. As he ambled through Garden City. As someone passed by him in the street, riding atop a rustic donkey cart, donkey hooves clip-clopping, bells singing sweetly. But in an instant, no longer than it takes thunder to clap, his sense of control left him.

What triggered Rossie's sudden sense of foreboding, of terror? Was it a certain street scent in a city known for its distinctly unpleasant odors? Or was it a sound, something contained in the white-noised cacophony at a busy intersection? Or was the origin of Rossie's dis-ease instead within his own head, a thought perhaps, just a thought? Whatever the cause, of one thing he was now certain: Beneath the beautiful embassy row neighborhood of Garden City lurked a disturbing malevolence equipped with secret underground passages and men with long knives and revolvers. Appearances as we know can be misleading.

As he walked, he reviewed what brought him to this place. Years of benign scholarship and off-the-beaten-track tourism should have been enough for him. Why had he allowed himself to be recruited into this shadowy world? No sooner had he mouthed the question than the answer rang in his head. "Revenge." For himself, and for his 24-year-old son, Kenneth Rossberg, Jr. Both men had endured survivors' hell at the hands of terrorists. Both men had stopped sleeping through their nights. During their days, when memories insisted on being heard, each man, in his way, fought a raging bitterness no amount of normal life seemed capable of repairing.

Rossie's "great adventure as international spy," so far, a stunning failure, was a reckless, some would say 'insane,' attempt to repair the damage, to gain restitution, for a crime heinous and final. Here to avenge his dear wife's horrible death.

That was why he was here on this eastern street, doing this questionable job.

So now, Rossie straightened his shoulders, shrugging off the feelings. Enough, he told himself. Get on with it. You are a man, damn-it! If an occasional unexplained kidnapping was the price for his mission, then so be it. "Be a man," he muttered, this time aloud. With those distinctly uncharacteristic macho thoughts,

Rossie headed for the hidden offices to keep his meeting, late only by a mere 18 hours.

As he approached his location, his fake story was all worked out. He was damned well not going to bring his boss into this. Besides, there was no 'this.' He was, after all, released, wasn't he? Mistakes happen, even among the odd bad lot. And with these thoughts, Rossie climbed the rickety wooden steps to the back entrance of a falling down office building, to a retinal scanner, to a waiting area where he was filmed. And finally, to his destination of the previous day.

Melvin Hibbard's office was as aluminum and bereft of personal effects as the man himself. 'Need to Know Melvin,' Rossie thought as he entered. The hooded eyes shielded a lifetime spent in The Company, giving nothing up in exchange finally for this position of authority commandeering U.S. intelligence inside Egypt.

"Unlike in academe, Professor, we in The Company like to keep our appointments and our commitments. Where the fuck were you yesterday? Mother was worried."

Spaghetti-O's. The distinct odor of Spaghetti-O's, as Rossie took his seat.

"I had a personal family matter that needed attention urgently, and I do apologize. I should have called."

Watching Melvin, the U.S.'s answer to overseas intelligence, lifting gloppy forkfuls of America's least favorite meal to his lips. Where does an American even get Spaghetti-O's in this town, he wondered. Rossie waited for the next salvo. For some reason he had taken a real disliking to this officious little man from the start.

"Well, according to your doorman, you were home by five. And according to your floor manager, you were in the bath after that. Couldn't have been such a large emergency. Plus, there are no call records on your cell, or your secure line."

Melvin's heavily lidded eyes watched Rossie's reaction as a lizard on a rock about to take a hapless insect as his next meal. No need to rush this. The outcome was predetermined.

"Look," began Rossie, who clearly needed to take a better tack, "the truth is I received a letter several days ago from the son in New York." He thought adding the word "the" in an impersonal fashion would play well to his audience. As Melvin paused his fork mid-bite, the better to listen, Rossie tried his best to appear the hapless family man.

"He thinks I'm someplace stateside in training, and after all this time, he is starting to challenge me and this job, is all. I handled it, but I needed time to think things through."

Rossie watched Melvin closely trying to gauge his boss's reaction to his claptrap.

"The Company wants family harmony, of course. And the off-spring . . . "

Rossie noted Melvin's impersonal tone. Good, he'd used the right approach.

". . .need to have confidence in their fathers' careers."

Rossie worked hard to maintain an even facial expression as, with a conspiratorial wink, Melvin finished the matter.

"We in the Company sometimes have to stick together. Civilians aren't cut out for this work. I, for one," –now warming to his subject, great, it worked -- "would keep them all in the dark. My experience with so-called 'truth-telling' Well . . ."

Melvin's voice trailed off in a cloud of espionage camaraderie. Rossie breathed a sigh of relief.

"Now, then, do not let it happen again. Understand?"

Rossie nodded solemnly.

Finally, wiping his greasy fingers on a sheet of crumpled up tissue, Melvin turned to the real business. "Tell me about your preliminary findings."

42

Karen Hagestad Cacy

7

Rossie drew a quick breath and began sharing
what he had learned in his latest round of coffee house
listening's, ever aware that his paycheck and Melvin's
continued success as 'Pooh-Bah' depended on the quantity
and quality of his findings.

Rossie's current debriefing was delivered against a
backdrop of limited successes by America in its long war
on terrorism. Earlier, renegades had been caught, their
nest of terrorists routed. But the Madrasa's of Pakistan,
Saudi Arabia, Iran, Yemen, and elsewhere had joined the
cause, training religion students in the politics of revenge
alongside the nobler tenets of Islam.

In other words, replacement troops were in situ,
set to go off at a moment's notice, at the drop of a cell
phone ring. Some scholars of terrorism focused on certain
nations, others on renegade mountain tribes, and still
others on known training camps. And rightly so.

But Melvin and his Spaghetti-O's were on a broader and far more complex assignment.

One might note the tomato stains gracing his polyester shirt front, identifying Melvin as a low-level pissant "Head of Mission" in some third world country in North Africa. But if one were a terrorist bent on the destruction of Western Civilization and its loosely held values, one would make such an assumption at one's peril. For Melvin's was a studied sloppiness, taken right out of the stagecraft archives of the CIA. A well-rehearsed front of ineptitude.

For today, Rossie was buying it. But very soon, (as today's impressions sank in?), Rossie would catch on to the act. Realize he was in deeper. See Melvin as a man of secrets, shadings, other purposes. Whose secrets? Whose shadings? What purposes? In time, in time.

For now, Melvin was all about a discreet order of business, that Rossie find one man: Fouad al Najimi. The target's shared dossier described a western- educated Palestinian. He was known to have spent a brief time in an Egyptian jail twenty years earlier for buzzing the capital city of Cairo in his Libyan Air Force F-16. Alcohol had helped the young pilot find sport in scaring tourists on camels out by Giza. The Libyans turned the upstart pilot over to the Egyptians for punishment.

Chastised, thrown in the clinker for a week, and out again. Did the young man gain certain insights during his brief trip through Egypt's penal system? There was no way to know. Yet having that information could help build a clearer understanding of the adult Fouad who was now under suspicion for far worse.

On the surface, his actions were little more than youthful pranks. At most, they showed an irreverent balance – social life, military service – each given equal parts of his time. The young pilot was a jokester who took part in car races along the narrow Delta road, drank liquor, and hosted his pals at his apartment in the desert, to the west of Cairo near the pyramids. Those were the days, my friend! Fouad's behavior might have mirrored any other twenty-something in the West. Parties. Girls. Pranks. Fun. It was practically the definition of young people the world over, their happy lives stretching before them. No worries. Just invincibility.

But was that all there was to this young blond, blue-eyed Palestinian air force pilot?

For now, 'Mr. Spaghetti-O's' was operating on a hunch: that an older and wiser Fouad quite possibly was Osama's heir, coordinating the show from state to state, village to village, tribe to tribe, even continent to continent. Certain cash accounts had been identified. Follow the money.

As yet unaware of Melvin's suspicions, Rossie began his report. "I have had my eye on three interesting men who regularly meet at a coffee shop next to the Khan el Khalili bazaar. From what I can gather, they met as classmates at American University here many years ago. They speak Arabic, mostly with Egyptian accents. French. English. Some German."

The lizard watched from hooded eyes. "Continue. Names please."

"Abdu. Fou Fou. And Ali, I believe."

"Obviously there was something that caught your attention." The lizard as interrogator.

"Secrecy. The way they shift easily into a particularly archaic and colloquial form of Arabic – a dialect used only by a certain Bedouin tribe that makes its home in the far reaches of Yemen's mountainous region. They have noticed me."

"And?"

"I believe they take me to be an Arab-American businessman, too westernized to know the finer points of their language. Their conversations have been fairly run-of-the-mill, typical of well-educated Arab men. They discuss women, in particular a belly dancer named "Aisha." Business. The usual rap on Israel and the West. I believe they live here in Cairo. Two are Egyptians and one is a Palestinian."

The Company had equipped Rossie with a clear plastic plug he wore in one ear, his curly, graying hair deflecting the eye from its presence. This marvelous device ensured the listener crystal clear sound from across even a crowded room. A certain cant of the listener's head was enough to provide the needed logarithmic coordinates. Thus, no one was safe from the interest of the Americans and their technologically advantaged partners. Of course, in this day and age of global reach, one could surmise that terrorists also were so aided in their listening habits.

Cat and mouse.

Rossie continued his report. "I have taken pains to speak slow, halting Arabic. And, of course, they speak very quickly, shifting easily between the Egyptian dialect with its hard "g," French, German, and then, as I mentioned, the more remote desert Arabic. During the last meeting, they kept referring to "Twelve" as though it were a man's name. Or an account number. Can't be sure. They were discussing international interest rates. An odd conversation given the Arab world's view of usury as a sin."

Melvin could take only so much of the professor in his ivory tower. "There's plenty that goes on here that doesn't pass that moral test . . . listen, I need more on these men. Stay on them until you can rule them in or out, understand?"

"The belly dancer, Aisha, dances at the

Shepheard's Hotel. Perhaps I could get to know her better. I think the Palestinian might be her lover, although she's considerably younger."

At this, Melvin let out a snort. "Professor, surely even within your ivy-covered buildings, the older man-younger woman scenario can't have escaped your attention. A pretty face? Come on, now!"

Rossie stared at a large bit of tomato sauce that had dropped onto Melvin's papers. Schmendrick.

Here we go, he thought.

What had he just proposed? Following a suspect's girlfriend? Even an ordinary, law-abiding man would object to such an incursion of privacy. But Rossie could see Melvin was already warming to the idea. He was not just pleased but titillated. So, it's come to this, he thought. Tracking belly dancers. Giving a sex-starved boss his reports. Possibly getting himself killed in the process. Briefly, he recalled how cold the revolver had been pressed against his back.

Melvin was off and running. "Excellent, Agent

Rossberg. You do that! But take care. Take care. Wouldn't want you being sent out to that place Amnesty International keeps reporting on, out in the Delta. Bad place to go. Heads are removed. So, take care, Agent Rossberg. Don't step in anything."

His handler continued. "Too bad we didn't give you more weaponry training. I'd hate to lose a speaker as skilled as you with so much important groundwork yet to do . . ."

Rossie grimaced at Melvin's total lack of personal feelings toward him. He was a human resource, nothing better than a higher form of early detection system. No more, no less. The form letter to his son to be sent upon his unfortunate loss was no doubt pre-signed with only the date left to be filled in later.

Melvin abruptly hit a button beneath his desk opening the door to his office. "Well then, off you go. We'll contact you in a few more days, see what you've learned."

Rossie left the office, nodding at a male receptionist outside the door. He walked down the long corridor. A second loud click opened a foot-thick door to the entrance atrium. Once inside the atrium, he awaited the third and final click that would release him back to the free and not so easy streets of downtown Cairo.

As he waited there, Melvin's disembodied voice came over a speaker in the hallway.

"Oh, uh, by the way, Rossberg. One last thing before you leave. The Company has information there's a bunch a bad guys on the loose downtown, harassing foreigners. Their M.O. is to wear women's black gallabiyah robes and they move in groups. Watch out for them. Lemme know if you happen upon them."

This startling announcement was immediately accompanied by an exceedingly loud door click releasing Rossie back to the rickety steps of the raggedy building. A meeting like no other.

52

8

Rossie began his work. He researched a belly dancer performing under the stage name of 'Aisha.' He heard her name mentioned several times by the three men at the coffee shop. Based on their conversations, he surmised it must be the Palestinian, Fouad al Najimi, she was dating.

The ever-helpful Melvin supplied him with written documents, a by-product of America's unique working relationship with Egypt's secret police. Certain tasks were regularly shared between the two countries. . . research, passport control, rendition, torture . . . as per a simple agreement among friends. An agreement that supplied a certain American with tomato sauce stains on his shirt with a written dossier covering a local belly dancer. 'It's no problem, Sayid Hibbard. No problem at all.'

Rossie was stunned by Melvin's dossier. Aisha

met Fouad when both were students at Princeton
University. Aisha was really 'Anne Kellogg,' daughter of
a wealthy American Fortune 500 insurance executive.
Her origins were far from the Middle East. Rather Anne's
origins were Scots-Irish, Norwegian, and English. Looks
can be deceiving. Her black hair and tawny skin perhaps
were a throwback to some distant relative who strayed
from the Anglo reservation. Her eyes, focused on one
Palestinian refugee, were an arresting shade of Tahoe
blue. Her curves when set in the hypnotic motion of the
belly dance could move any man to tears. But she danced
only for one.

The report continued: She was known to be fluent
in Arabic and French, courtesy of her schooling and travel
to the Middle East. Choosing not to complete her
university studies, Anne chose instead a life course that
finally brought her to Cairo's Shepheard's Hotel as a
headline entertainer.

Only the wealthy trafficked at Corniche El Nile in
the heart of Cairo's Garden City, home of the historic
hotel. The hotel's guests going all the way back to its
founding in 1841 reflected a virtual tapestry of North
Africa -- its wars, culture clashes, and geopolitical

decisions. Those taking tea in the hotel's grand lobby over the years included British soldiers, Red Chinese adventurers, French mercenaries, Italian counts, Belgian diamond merchants, American military officers, German archaeologists, African princes, Persian Gulf potentates, and an Iranian Shah or two. Smoothing their way was a plethora of beautiful women practicing the seductive art of belly dancing. Midst the potted palms, state secrets were shared, teacups passed, and certain men's eyes were, year in and year out, predictably trained on the beautiful dancers as they arrived to dress for evening performances.

Tonight, it was no different. Rossie always loved sitting in Shepheard's elegant atrium, sipping strong Egyptian tea and observing the international set as they moved about. Suddenly, all heads turned as a strong scent of Jasmine perfume floated by. The eyes, up-turned and almond shaped, had no need of heavy make-up. The black lashes were more than enough. The red painted lips, however, signaled, 'Aisha,' your performer for the evening. Hide the children.

Rossie strained to hear her as she addressed the desk clerk and then the concierge in Arabic. Her accent, from what little he heard, was excellent. He noticed that she used the hard Egyptian "G" over the softer "G' used in other dialects.

Rossie took his time entering the restaurant for a late dinner. He did his best to adopt the look of a bored executive, tired of the insufficiencies of the Egyptian culture. He tried to curl his lip disdainfully. Instead, on this spy, the look came off more as a facial tic. What an idiot. As the wine warmed him, Rossie dropped his pretense and allowed himself to enjoy the fine food and elegant surroundings.

In due course, he befriended some other Americans whom he joined for Aisha's act in the lounge after dinner. No one, of course, had heard Rossie's expert Cairene accent. All they heard was a loud American, getting into the evening. His eyes and ears, however, were trained on the trio of Arab men seated up front in the VIP section. He noted that the Palestinian's two partners used great caution in their demeanor towards the talent. This was obviously Fouad's girl. There were boundaries. It wouldn't do to intrude on their friend's turf.

In the Arab world, demeanor means everything. Nomads encamped at a desert oasis customarily greet travelers with warmth, offering food and drink. Once the visitor leaves the wadi however, he might get his throat slit. But never in his host's presence at dinner. Manners are manners. And customs are customs. Tonight, in Shepheard's Hotel as well.

Aisha was good. One would never guess her American background. She had the moves down, and was increasingly seductive, swaying with the music. So sexy and inviting were her moves, that some of the American women in the audience actually blushed. When would they see fit to entertain their men? Never, was the pristine answer. Athletic bodies were one thing. But undulating hips and lowered lashes, quite another. Thankfully, the women watched as Aisha's special Arab men guests led in the wild applause. Good, their husbands would never step over that line. The beautiful Aisha was taken. That much was clear. They would, later however, need to deal with a certain up-tick in their spouses' lustiness. Ah, the price of foreign travel.

9

Rossie left the hotel in an alcohol-induced fog. Separation from his current state of mind seemed fitting and appropriate, something someone owed him. He strolled along the Corniche by the Nile. Soft night air, the distant song of donkey carts, and Rossie's failure to be on guard made the watermelon seller's job easy. He inched his cart closer as Rossie took a seat on an empty bench.

As Rossie would be the first to admit, there was little to study. His life really wasn't all that complicated. The circumstances, yes, complicated as hell. The genesis of those circumstances? Pretty straightforward and believable.

How does a civilian American find himself in Cairo reporting to the likes of Melvin? If he is in this circumstance, shouldn't he have a gun? Shouldn't he be a Navy Seal, trained in urban combat? At a minimum, shouldn't he have worked his way up the ranks of his nation's spy network? A man, perhaps, who walks funny, but who, in actuality knows how to kill in many ingenious ways? A man with state-of-the-art security devices at his command? As he reached for his phone to call New York, Rossie noticed a well-dressed man had taken a seat at the end of the bench. The man caught his eye and began speaking.

"Do you speak Arabic?" He asked in Arabic.

Rossie adopted a confused expression and answered in English. He could not speak Arabic, 'un peu de francais.' Sorry.

The man continued in Arabic as though Rossie had not spoken.

"It's a lovely evening. There is no place on earth quite like Cairo. I do much business in Saudi Arabia. I can tell you, Cairo and Beirut are so much better. Many more cultural events. Freedom to do what one chooses. Not so much fundamentalism. Islam. It's not such a bad religion, you know. It has simply suffered from -- how do you say it in English? " --

Here, the man switched to English: "Bad press."

He continued on in Arabic. "Westerners do not understand our culture. Even your reporters and government people who visit are clueless. It's a pity that Americans are so arrogant. They think they can come to our land and learn of things. Chase people they do not know. Search for our innermost secrets. Some believe, because they have attended prestigious universities, they understand. They study our language. They affect analysis. But they are wrong. And they will never succeed. They need to stay home where they belong. Leave us. Leave us all in peace for a change. A- bientot,, monsieur."

With those words, the stranger rose to go. He stopped briefly near the watermelon cart. Rossie watched as he murmured something to the seller, then purchased a piece of fruit and walk away. Rossie heard the creak of the cart as it passed behind him and out of sight. Long after the evening's shadows swallowed up the man, he could still hear the music of the cart's bell, marking his departure.

Rossie stared at the city lights reflecting off of one

of the world's longest rivers, a river that connected Africa to itself in much the same way that Rossie's current assignment connected Rossie to himself. It made sense, if you knew the details. 'The devil is in the details.'

Revenge. He was here for revenge. For Rachel. And again, she was on his mind. Her last night on earth was on his mind.

10

Most modern world capitals like Cairo are lodged in civilization's oldest settlements. Current city centers are clogged with traffic, commerce, and visitors. Here, deals are made. Passports are checked and re-checked. Each city possesses its own distinct urban core. A place where people live and work, each day. Down each street are familiar faces. In the bakery shop. At the newsstand. In the coffee shop. That same man, or woman, arrives at a set time and place each day. Creatures of habit, even the least of us may be recognized as we go about our business in these crowded urban villages. It is well- nigh impossible to remain unknown for long, even in Cairo, one of the world's most populated cities.

The day after her performance, as was her habit, Aisha slept late. Fouad did not live with her in her small Garden City apartment, although his books and clothing were strewn about everywhere as if he did. Rising about ten, as was her custom, she made her way to Groppi's coffee shop downtown for her first cup of coffee and a glance at the International Herald tribune.

She particularly searched for news from home. Even a home invasion in Connecticut caught her attention, so great sometimes was her homesickness. Any news would do in a pinch. In the same way, she searched faces on city streets for fellow Americans. One nationality always can tell another. There is an unwritten code. The way they move. An attitude. Americans always stood out to each other.

Aisha remembered the short American man who attended her performance the evening before. Today, she realized he too was a regular late coffee shop habitué. And here he was again as on so many other mornings. There was something introspective about the man. He clearly was not receptive to being approached, that much she could tell.

There was something else. She thought he might be watching her. It would not be surprising. Once western men caught one of her shows, their eyes would follow her when she was recognized. Every man wanted his own Aisha to love. Why not this small man as well, reading his paper?

The two strangers continued reading their English language newspapers and drinking their sweet dark coffees at separate tables. Their informal watching of each other had begun. Rossie now knew who she was. She was his link to Fouad al Najimi. She lived in Rossie's world. She was a regular predictable person. Easy to watch. As with most of us, she could be found on any given day according to her routine.

Today, Rossie had a plan: 'Professor as professional tracker.' He left the coffee shop ahead of her and ducked into a corner alleyway and waited for her to come out. Finally, she emerged from the shop and made her way on foot to Garden City, not ten blocks from Tahrir Square. He carefully followed her as she strolled along the Corniche, as she stopped at a small vegetable cart. Later Rossie watched her enter a six-story pension on Sharia Kasr el Aini. Through the ornate glass and wrought iron front door, he could see her collect mail from a box using a key.

Melvin would be pleased. He wondered if terrorists knew each other. Wasn't that Melvin's point?

Track this al Najimi character and the others would be close by? With the full strength of the American clandestine community at his back, Rossie would locate his own terrorist. For a personal transaction. He wondered if he would be caught. Would he be extradited to America, or would they deal with him at that place near Alexandria? Would someone behead him? In the Middle East, after all, beheading can be an acceptable resolution. These are the matters that engaged the professor's thoughts. Also, a reminder to himself to visit the American gun range in the Nile Delta. To get ready.

11

Ismailia, Suez Canal, Summer '64

The six twenty-somethings ran around Egypt all summer. The three American girls, Rachel, Lorna, and Susie, were summer students at American University in Cairo, off on their first worldly adventure. And their dates, three local men, Fouad – 'Fou Fou,' Ali, and Abdullah – 'Abdu,' were recent AUC graduates. The men and women were innocent, giddy with life, and having a summer like no other.

Dancing in clubs, hiking in the desert, shopping in the Cairo bazaar, drinking crème de menthe by the Nile. The soft desert air blessed their youthful adventures. A bubble of young life enveloped them. Nothing could harm them. No one could be them. This was their time. The summer was a perfect beginning for magical futures. Their youthful invincibility was so strong it fairly crackled. As they passed others, their excitement at being alive was contagious. "Happiness" in the dictionary would forever carry a picture of the six mugging for the camera.

Yet . . .

. . . there were signs of trouble. Rachel's bags were packed at all times. She was trailed by American agents, who at a moment's notice could whisk her safely from the country. While she appeared to most observers to be an ordinary, slightly giddy twenty-year old, full of college high jinx, in Cairo she also could be a potential target of international terrorists. She was the Jewish girl, taking a chance on Egypt.

But she was having a great time as Egypt welcomed her with arms flung open. The country did not disappoint. No dark strangers lurked in the shadows ready to seize her. No one threatened her. Quite the opposite. Only smiling faces, intrigued with the American girl speaking passable colloquial Arabic in the French clubs of the Moquattam Hills.

Very simply, she was, as the others, a happy-go-lucky tourist. An impetuous college student, off on an exotic adventure in North Africa. The one odd note was that her date, Fouad al Najimi, was Palestinian. She happily embraced him along with her studies of Arabic and her classes in Islamic Civilization. Ma'aleesh. There was no problem between them. From their first meeting, the two were drawn to each other. Her bubbly personality was a perfect foil for his more somber, 'world weary' demeanor. Always the gentleman, Fouad held doors, spoke softly, and was solicitous of his American friend.

The time was late August nearing the end of her stay in Egypt. Rachel was just back from a tour of Abu Simbel in southern Egypt. "Fou Fou. We have to talk."

"Of course, Rachel. What is it?"

Fouad was a mere three years her senior. But he possessed the steady presence of mind that reminded Rachel of her step-father, a famous lawyer. Both men were unflappable, sincere, quiet. She felt safe with Fou Fou. His judgment was that of someone much older and wiser.

Rachel sat up to her full five- foot, four- inch height to deliver her important news: "Fou Fou, I am Jewish."

"Yes. So?" His reaction was not what she expected. Where was the outrage? The political lecture? The expected withdrawal?

"Well . . . I mean . . . you are Palestinian. Doesn't this concern you?"

"Are you a Zionist?"

He invoked the name of a political movement dedicated to expanding Israel by encroaching on Palestinian lands. A continuation of the conflict.

"No, probably not."

"Then we don't have a problem."

With that assurance, Fou Fou took Rachel's hand and walked her to the banks of the Suez to show her Egypt's fleet of defense camels. There, in a corral, were about twenty laconic camels. In case of trouble, he proudly announced, these camels would be employed in Egypt's national defense. The absolute seriousness of his account was stunning. He really was proud of these camels. It was such moments of simple innocence that drew Rachel closer to Fou Fou. A camel defense battalion?

Who would be proud of such a thing? Her Fou Fou, was the answer.

Later back in the U.S., as Rachel was confronted with a barrage of harsh media accounts of ongoing Middle East conflicts, Fou Fou's friendship and the summer of '64 were never far from her mind. She collected camels. She voraciously monitored news accounts of the region. Finally, unable to tear herself away, she became a scholar of Islamic culture.

Never did she desert her own. Her strong Jewish identity and faith served her well throughout her life. But her tribal home within the Old Testament, the Torah, was tempered by her Egyptian experience. Never would Fou Fou be far away from her heart.

A summer lover, far away in time and space. Nevertheless, a man of substance. Her Fou Fou.

72

12

Rachel Rossberg made a post-middle age bucket list decision. She would return to Cairo, with her two girlfriends. The three shared their early twenties in that city, as they attended the American University. They dated three Arab friends: Ali, Fouad and Abdullah. Belly dancers danced for the six friends as they sipped gin and tonics at Cairo's international dinner clubs . . . they climbed the pyramids by moonlight . . . danced to the latest French ballads in a supper club overlooking the desert . . . visited a beach house near Ismailia in northern Egypt . . . sunbathed at the infamous British country club, Nadi Gezira . . .bought French bikinis . . . had their ears pierced . . . .rode horses to a desert home lit only by candles . . . swam across the Suez Canal to see Egypt's herd of 'Civil Defense' camels in a stable nearby . . . . and laughed as their three dates comically kidded each other, now in Arabic, next in French, and often in the King's English. Rachel and her friends filled the spaces between their Arabic studies very nicely indeed.

This time, with memories soaring and more credit cards and means in their wallets than on their first trip to Cairo, the three traveled on a cruise ship. Their cabins were plush, with a balcony high above the Mediterranean Sea passing beneath them. As the three traveled back in time they wondered what would they find there? Former lovers? Perhaps. What else? Their imaginations ran wild as the ship made its steady way to Alexandria.

The weather, as it turned out, was perfect. No oceanic storms marred their long-dreamed about vacation. Instead, the three women led by Rachel, enjoyed more than a few mixed drinks as they made passage back to the desert and their own pasts.

Life is always better in one's twenties. Mistakes are made, to be sure. But youth cloaks it all in a dream world of the possible. Life stretches before us when we're young, as it did that summer in Cairo for Rachel. Early in life, anticipation runs high. For a life filled with loves, happiness, and the promise of all wonderful things.

It happened their last night at sea, at a location somewhere west of Alexandria. At first they thought the

ship was in distress. But how could that be? The seas
were calm, the passage uneventful. Passengers were
called from their cabins in the night, most already in night
clothes. Rachel was cold, having forgotten in her panic,
to grab her robe.

Topside, passengers were greeted by an army of
terrorists dressed in camouflage, carrying long, dangerous
looking rifles. The ship's crew was tied and on their
knees, looking appropriately terrified. Their eyes
apologized to their passengers. They had tried their best
to save the ship. They had fought. They had radioed for
help. But now, here they all were anyway. In a black
oceanic night.

To Rachel, a Jewish scholar of Arabic and its
numerous dialects, their purpose was instantly clear. They
were going to terrorize them, make the world's headlines,
and supposedly, gain sympathy for their cause, returning
Palestine to its former pre-Ben Gurion status.

It went on for hours. It did not end well for many.
But Rachel never knew all that happened that fateful
night. Because instantly, her Sephardic appearance, not to
mention her Star of David necklace, caused separation

from the other passengers. She understood every word the men said. She heard their studly cackling. She understood their issue. At some level, she even could agree with parts of their argument.

Did she answer them in Arabic? Passengers who survived the attack later thought they heard her speaking, but the oceanic winds drowned out her words. After only a few moments, the head terrorist grabbed at her gold necklace, ripping it from around her neck. Then, he and another man roughly lifted her over the ship's railing, tossing her into the dark, churning ocean below.

The men kept her necklace, as a souvenir for their boss back on land. See what we did? See what we brought you? Like cats carrying dead birds in their jaws, proudly showing off their prey. What brave kitties. What a great bunch of men. For the cause. Without hesitation.

Rachel lost her life. And in that horrible moment, her gentle scholarly husband, waiting back home in New York, Kenneth L. Rossberg, Sr., 'Rossie,' lost his. Nothing could ever be the same. A death, any death, serves as a benchmark for the living, those left behind. But such a horrid, terror-filled death? A marker for the survivors, altering their lives and perceptions forever.

Since that fateful night aboard the Italian cruise ship, Rossie's life, and that of his only son, Kenneth L. Rossberg, Jr., were maelstroms of sorrow mixed with anger. The two men never knew they could possess such hatred for people they had never met. Rachel's murderers.

Revenge brought Rossie to this night by the Nile River, seated atop a fulcrum of seething hatred, with danger on one side and heartbreak on the other. There was no way out. No right way to fall. He needed to call his son stateside. . .. touch the anchor of family. Later, he would look her murderer in the eye . . . much later.

13

Rossie and Rachel's only son was an attractive young man. Kenneth Rossberg, like his father and mother, was an excellent student. Private schools paved his way to the Ivy League, and now he was just beginning a promising career as an attorney in one of New York's mid-range law firms. He dated women, but no one stayed long enough to make it to the ring ceremony. Nevertheless, Kenneth was on track for an illustrious life. However, his mother's untimely death, the international publicity that followed the event, and his father's crazy new government sabbatical to Egypt, had sent his plans into a tailspin.

At first Ken, Jr. dealt with grief, then anger at his mother's murder. But he also was facing a father's mid-life rage and inexplicable need to change career paths to the Middle East. What was next? A red Ferrari? Early onset Alzheimer's Disease? In a word, Ken was worried sick about his father. All he had been told was that his father would be working as an Arabic/Hebrew translator, working for the U.S. State Department based in Cairo. That he would be on temporary leave from his fine university where his tenure as Islamic scholar was firm and lasting.

But Ken knew his father's torment was even greater than his own, which was considerable. His father needed to be at home in New York, surrounded by familiar things, reading, writing and healing. Together, the two men could get past their loss. But continents apart? Not bloody likely.

14

Rossie had no choice but to seek out his mentor again. It was becoming apparent that in Rossie's tenuous world, Melvin was the closest thing to a friend he had at present. Back to Spaghetti-O's and duplicity. The American lizard sitting on his rock, flicking his tongue. But, Melvin as sympathetic boss? The image gave Rossie a chill.

So be it. There was, after all, Rossie's personal mission, as yet undisclosed to his estimable employer, to be considered. The Company might have been using Rossie. But Rossie was also using the Company for his own purposes.

Did Rossie really think Melvin was unaware of his situation? That Rachel's death had played no role in the Company's recruitment of him? That Melvin and his spy buddies really cared two cents about Rossie or his son?

Now, however, it appeared that Rossie's role as the Company's eyes and ears on the ground was compromised. He gave Melvin the news. Obviously, the three men knew Rossie's identity. Their warning was clear. But at the same time, he could report real progress – he could tell Melvin where al Najimi's girlfriend lived.

"So." Melvin leaned back in his chair looking at his ceiling. Then he punched a button on his computer.

Rossie's voice from the night before came back to him clearly:

" .. . 'un peu de francais'"

And then, the man's Arabic response: "'It's a lovely evening. There is no place on earth quite like Cairo. I do much business in Saudi Arabia. I can tell you, Cairo and Beirut are so much better.'"

Melvin switched off his little spy recorder. His hand went up, in his signal to Rossie that some thought process or other was underway. The lizard, thinking. Rossie listened to the man's clock ticking. Somewhere in the distance, a secretary answered a phone.

"You are new to this world, Professor Rossberg. I have failed you to an extent. We had our reasons. We had hoped that your persona was such that you might be able to travel under the radar. That is in fact why you were hired. We gave it a try. No offense, but the 'post middle-aged professor' bumbling his way through Cairo," was more our thought.

Melvin continued his reverie. "Do you recall visiting the embassy here about ten years ago? We had an attractive young lady, blonde hair, blue eyes, kinda' breathy, baby doll voice, working as receptionist. She was the first person everyone saw as they visited. You would remember her, believe me!"

Settle in, it's story-time.

"No one, not even her fellow employees, knew her real name."

America's Chief of Station continued, shrewd now, wanting to share with Rossie a bit of his well-considered professionalism. What he knew. His powers as U.S. spy chief.

"She was, in fact, your government's answer to the very image of a 'dumb blonde.' You know how Arabs love blonde women. Follow 'em down the street. Engage them in conversation. The Nordic type sets their hearts all aquiver. Cuts right through their protective layers. We know that. 'Course no one knew she was fluent in Arabic, including her workers at the embassy. Damned clever placement, if you ask me."

Melvin was enjoying himself. Why interrupt?

He droned on. "Once, we had her listening in on a phone conversation between a coupla' suspects. The conversation turned to the ordinary. Our heroine was absent mindedly trimming her hair as she listened. By accident, she cut her own phone cord. Your government at work! Funny story. But it should illustrate to you your own situation. This young woman was effective for us."

Rossie and Melvin were pals, sharing a good story over a beer.

"One time though, they picked her up and threw her in jail. They said she was a spy. Even then, they couldn't make their way past her demure, feminine appearance. Over several days, they kept asking her -- in English, of course -- why was she in Cairo? You want to know what bothered them though? You think it was the so-called spying?"

Here, a conspiratorial chuckle.

"Those bastards simply could not make their way past the idea of such an attractive woman of her age being unmarried. No husband. No children. They found it odd and disturbing. Not to mention a damned waste. Finally, after three or four days, they released her back to the U.S. Embassy. Clean as a whistle. A woman beyond reproach. They checked and found nothing. Only their own desires staring them in the mirror. A blonde woman. What treasure to have her in their holding cell if only for a brief while!"

"Of course, we were squawking all along. The same story, her cover: 'She is a simple girl making her living here, as a government secretary. Let her go. Are you mad, to hold such a sweet woman?'"

Finishing . . .

"Of course, they agreed with us. She fit their stereotype, so they let her go. I dare say, they served her tea and crumpets each afternoon, so as not to offend. I believe she is now living out West, married to a nice building contractor. But she was extremely useful, I can tell you"

Finally tying his story back to Rossie, Melvin was nothing, if not efficient: ". . .and that was what we had hoped from you."

And here, Melvin went too far, so delighted was he with his own cleverness:

"Oh, not in a dumb blonde persona, understand. A different face. You would be our inept, myopic scholar of a certain age, in Cairo for a good time . . . a naïve, grieving husband, too broken for western society, who has headed out to the Middle East to escape himself. Perhaps a man who drinks a bit much. Obviously, a man who is coping rather poorly in his life. A man, of course, beyond reproach, a man terribly unlikely to target anyone. Hell, a man who can't even shoot straight. And, yes, to answer your question, I have seen your scores from the shooting range."

Rossie could feel the bile rising in his throat at Melvin's description of him. Then, somewhere in his head, a funny picture appeared. He was wearing a blonde Marilyn Monroe wig, wearing a trench coat, chasing bad guys with a gun clenched in his hand.

The humor caused him a kind of separation from the lizard on his rock. Who the hell did Melvin think he was, anyway? Rossie was credentialed. A tenured college professor, linguist par excellence, he could as easily set out on his own. Accomplishing what exactly, remained unclear. But the path at least would be his path, having fewer ties to the U.S. State Department or any of Melvin's other 'compadres.'

There. The settlement had come. Rossie had come to terms jarred from his unsuccessful spy work by Melvin's casual insensitivity.

Had Melvin gone too far? Apparently, he had gone just far enough. Far enough to allow Rossie to regain his bearings. To retake his life, his own sense of justice, outrage and need for revenge. Time to leave the

U.S. government's fine employ. As these thoughts tumbled into existence, seemingly from a distance, he heard Melvin's conclusion.

"And now . . . now . . . you may as well return to New York. They know. They know."

Rossie began to speak, but Melvin raised his hand signaling he was not finished.

"As of now, I am placing you in a new category, Rossberg. No more watching. I will be sending you on smaller more targeted assignments from here on out. I want you to expand your personal life. Write a book or something, whatever it is you professors do. Do that. Lay low for a while. Later, I'll contact you for something small. Something that will assist us in our mission but will be completely within your new more innocent life. As to your future tasks . . . I'll be sending you on more jobs in keeping with your more cerebral limits. Understand?"

Rossie had to admit the man had a way with words. Did he speak to everyone the same way? Still, the professional seated in his Brink's truck of an office had

spoken. Rossie's new assignment was easily done.
Temporarily stand down. Drink wine. 'Do whatever it is
you professors do.' You had to love Melvin. America's
fortress of sophistication.

Yet, Rossie and Melvin finally agreed on
something. He was no spy. He knew that. Melvin knew
it. Hell, certain kidnappers in Garden City Cairo even
knew that. He recalled their derisive laughter. Then,
something else came into focus: the orange the woman
inexplicably placed in his hand before shoving him into
the street.

Besides that memory, another joined it. He
recalled Fouad's dossier. The man's odd obsession with
oranges. Was it Fouad's men who forced him into the
back seat of a car that day in Garden City? Even the
disgraced and recently demoted so-called 'spy' could
begin to see a connection between the two memories.
Rossie's realization opened up a new avenue of thinking
and paranoia. Why bring Melvin onboard at this late
date? Hadn't he just been cut loose anyway? Ma'aleesh.

The tables were turned now anyway. Rossie had
his own work to do, and it most certainly did not include

writing a book. He needed to lay his own groundwork. Because he intended to deliver his feeling of rage personally and to the correct party. Fouad al Najimi, 'the orange man,' was quickly rising to the top of Rossie's list of suspects.

Nothing to see here. Move along, folks. Rossie thought of Churchill's statement during World War II: "Never give up." A man to emulate. Winston Churchill.

15

The college professor as student. One is never too old to learn. Rossie returned to his small apartment in Garden City to contemplate his next move. He began by calling his son.

The father who had not set foot inside a synagogue since Rachel's funeral began with an uncharacteristic question: "Have you been observant, son?"

"Dad?"

"Look. It's none of my business. I was just thinking, being in the community, being observant, might help, given everything."

"Help, Dad? Oh, you mean help get over mom's murder by terrorists. Or maybe you mean help get over the fact that my dad's run off to Egypt, scene of the crime.'

"We both are dealing with this in our own ways, son. I know it's been hard."

Rossie reached for the gin bottle on his kitchen counter. And poured. His son could hear the clink of ice cubes against a glass. The non-verbal's between the two men often conveyed more than their conversations.

"So, what are you really doing? I can't believe you went all that way to put your tenure on hold and translate what some bums in Cairo are saying. You need to tell me what's really going on. How stupid do you think I am, Dad?!"

Rossie should have known Kenneth wouldn't accept his story. What now?

"That's not it. You know . . . your mother was very close to this country. I have . . . have been following her footsteps. I know it sounds weird. But I feel closer to her here than in New York. I hope you can understand. There is an end in sight, I assure you. But for now . . ."

Rossie's voice trailed off as Kenneth heard him take a long sip of his drink.

"Alright, Dad. I get it. Take your time. But then get the hell back here."

"I love you Kenneth. We are all we have now. You know, it's about time you got serious about finding your own life partner. Any progress in that department?"

Rossie always felt uncomfortable discussing Kenneth's personal life. Rossie's own awkwardness when it came to the opposite sex affected his ability to advise his far handsomer son. The boy always had girls after him. Somehow, however, none of them had been the real deal.

Kenneth couldn't believe his father's quick shift back to the real world. A world where eligible bachelors date, marry, have children. Purchase retirement plans. Oh, that life.

"Not so much, Dad. Look, uh, I need to get back to work now. I love you."

Before Rossie could respond, he heard a click as his son hung up the phone. He reached for the gin.

Back in New York, Kenneth knew his dad was knocked off balance. He was relieved to learn his dad's trip was really about his mother. Scholasticism aside, he always had had difficulty understanding his parents' strange ties to the Middle East. While those ties had gotten his mother murdered, he knew his dad would need to reconcile his life of Islamic scholarship with that hard fact. In a strange way, if one discounted the alcohol, his father seemed to be on the mend. If it took living in far off Cairo for a while longer, so be it.

His conversation with Kenneth completed, Rossie stood on his balcony overlooking the Corniche, drink in hand. Donkey bells jingled on a passing food cart. A muezzin called the faithful to prayer. An innocent evening in a one-off world capital. Once one has been to Cairo, the city is in one's blood forever. Perhaps it even alters one's DNA. The soft air, endless sunsets, and traces of ancient culture combine to create a cocktail as difficult to resist as a special woman, her perfume lingering not a day, but a lifetime.

Cairo.

On his fourth drink, Rossie turned his attention inward. The weight of recent intrigues and fears temporarily was held at bay by the alcohol. Eventually, even a simple college professor could put this one together. Melvin had taped his conversations. Meaning, anything he said anywhere in this city was fair game for "The Company's" eager ears.

He was not alone. For Rossie, that empirical knowledge had its upside and its obvious downside. What a government, with its technological advances! Could they glean his thoughts as well?

Equally troubling was Melvin's story about the government's blonde so-called 'asset.' Rossie's introduction to the dark side of espionage was supported by no such manufactured identity. Everyone knew his name from the start. . . his real name . . . the name that was yelled from the roof tops as the world's newspapers covered the stunning story of Rachel's death a year earlier.

What now was clear to him was that he had been served up as fodder for his own country. Not only was he not camouflaged for his new assignment in Cairo, he'd been *paraded*. He was the bait. Not the searcher, but the searched.

Now, however, he no longer owed allegiance to them. But thanks to them, his entry to Cairo had been noted by *everyone*. He was identified, located, and tagged - by all sides. There was another way to view his situation: his course was now obvious -- all he had to do was wait. When they were ready, the bastards would come to him.

A block away, the ageless Nile flowed on, its knowledge intact. The river beckoned to Rossie; he listened carefully. 'Go to the Nile. Let life's tides float by. Relax. Take a break.' Perhaps the world and its evils – Rachel's murderers – could wait a while longer.

16

Sausalito, California, three years earlier

Rossie once took a floating home tour to view Sausalito's storied houseboat community. There, the houseboats' flower-festooned verandas sat perched high above the water, with strong Pacific currents passing underneath. The community's fortunate residents greeted each sunset from those verandas, drinks in hand.

Make no mistake: the houseboat residents' work was cut out for them. They needed to monitor pelicans as they fished for their dinner, to greet and feed greedy sea lions en route to Fishermen's Wharf. They needed to stir themselves periodically to refill drink glasses and stoke barbeque grills. They needed to concentrate on Mother Nature, to feed the neighbor's cat, perhaps to adjust a rubber bumper guard that had come loose between dock and houseboat. They needed to direct their gaze to the famous San Francisco skyline, to tall building spires floating above the fog bank, making the city appear as a magical version of "Oz."

These tasks were important ones. And houseboat denizens took their responsibilities very seriously.

Following Rossie's tour, the idea that a tranquil life could be achieved by living on the water was firmly planted, providing him an imaginary escape. The worse his life became, and lately it had become very bad indeed, the more Rossie found himself floating off to San Francisco Bay, drink in hand. He never told anyone of his thoughts, not even Rachel. It was Rossie's private fantasy, known only to him. The thought of such a life served to calm him, to give him hope when the lights around him dimmed. Somehow, now seemed to be the time . . . the time to merge his dreams with reality. The time to recreate himself. The time to escape everyone, especially his former self.

A casual observer might posit that a move to Cairo for a middle- aged college professor already signaled such an escape. But for Rossie, who by now had spent years of his research life in Middle Eastern capitals, Cairo was familiar turf. Now he needed more. He needed the dream. Reality hadn't been working out so well of late. It was fantasy-time.

Newly released from assigned responsibilities, as he went out, Rossie no longer took as much care with his words. His fluent excellent Arabic served him well . . . in the Khan el Khalili Bazaar, the local coffee shops, and on street corners. Eventually, he was shown the way to the man in charge of all things 'waterfront.'

Rossie made his way to the river of life . . . for Africa and himself. He felt as though he was sleeping-walking. Like T. E. Lawrence (of Arabia,) another dreamer: "All men dream, but not equally. Those who dream by night in the dusty recesses of their minds, wake in the day to find that it was vanity; but the dreamers of the day are dangerous men, for they may act on their dreams with open eyes, to make them possible."

On the one hand, Rossie sought the comfort and solace of water. On the other hand, he knew it wouldn't end well. Still, he couldn't let it go. For too long, he had been the dispassionate scholar sitting on the sidelines, watching others act out their dreams. And now his dreams had become nightmares. How far would this take him? When would he wake up?

17

The purveyor of Nile houseboats, it turned out, was a Swiss guy named 'Werner.'

Through a contact their meeting was arranged to take place in Groppi's Ice Cream Parlor in downtown Cairo. As Rossie entered the café, he searched the small round marble tables for the man who had been described to him – diminutive, European, carrying a leather 'man purse.'

There he was, as described . . . chain smoking ubiquitous French Gauloise cigarettes through a showy, highly illegal cigarette holder of carved elephant ivory.

The pale, blonde man seemed as much out of his element in Cairo as a desert nomad might in the Swiss Alps – he stood out immediately. He was nursing a small cup of thick black, hopelessly sweet, Egyptian coffee, reading the latest copy of the International Herald

Tribune. A pair of sunglasses were rakishly perched atop his head. Stateside, his impeccable attire and demeanor might have signaled "gay." Here in a more heterosexually repressive regime, where 'man-on-man' oddly was more common, it merely signaled "foreigner."

Modern Middle East history is filled with the flotsam and jetsam of human flight. An arid climate, magical deserts, crystalline nights, the unmistakable remoteness of these countries, all have served as catnip for certain types of individuals --novelists in sweet Moroccan exile, Brits out for nomadic adventure, French Foreign Legionnaires, ordinary eccentrics, archaeologists . . . and the occasional American scholar bent on payback.

As Rossie approached Werner, the man smoothed a pencil slim mustache and held out a limp hand.

As he sat down, Rossie thought, "Euro Trash."

The man greeted him warmly. Rossie knew the type – if you had the cash, he had the goods. The Swiss fop came well equipped with rental brochures, photographs, lease agreements. It was clear the sooner rent payments might begin, the better this man would like it. After the preliminaries – Rossie noticed an accent cloaked in a slight lisp – the two men made their way to the waterfront to view his properties.

As they approached the river, a sea bird swooped down and hovered in front of Rossie, flapping its wings. The thing cawed at him insistently. Rossie filled in its messages: 'Welcome to my waterfront! Beware! Do you serve almonds at the cocktail hour? Would Rachel like your new place? Are you drinking too much?'

And with one last caw, 'Are you sure you know what you're doing?'

18

**"Your old men will dream dreams, your
young men will see visions."**
Joel 11:28

Not far from Rossie's newly rented houseboat at the Nile's Corniche in Garden City, a Roman Catholic, blue-eyed Palestinian met the night with benefit of alcohol. The commonly held notion that Arabs don't drink, that the Middle East is 'dry,' would be news to the many proprietors of nightclubs and bars throughout the region.

With the benefit of whiskey, this particular Arab was contemplating a career course change. On account of Rachel's murder – his biggest mistake.

'Bless him father, for he has sinned.'

As terrorists go, to the extent their motivations are known, Fouad was located somewhere near the bottom. So far, there was only the one killing by his men, who had not yet come to grasp the difference between the other international terrorist, now summarily buried at sea by Navy Seals, and their new boss.

They were unaware their leader who was an intellectual international attorney, was guided by more strategic theories such as those contained in the 'Chinese Art of War.' He was not interested in bloodletting per se, only in results. His life experience brought him to the difficult realization that for those holding the ultimate weapon, respect was accorded. If not respect, at least the grudging accommodation of serious international diplomacy.

If at some time in the future, Palestinians could possess a weapon worthy of bringing the world's negotiators to the table, perhaps a deal would be struck. Finally, and all, homeland returned. Camps destroyed. Land reclaimed. Lives resurrected. Let Israel have its little nation. But also, let the world stop avenging Germany's past sins through the blood and treasure of those living half a world away.

Per his plan, Fouad set up the ship high jacking as a theatrical stunt to gain attention for his freedom fighters. As a statement of will and mission to focus the world's attention on their message: 'We are here. We mean business. Pay attention. Let us regain our destiny.'

For the mission, Fouad's men were overheated in the extreme. They self-medicated before the mission with a hashish/cocaine cocktail to calm their nerves, and ready themselves for the taking of the cruise ship. There was no prior thought of religious suicide. Their instructions were clear: no one was to get hurt.

Fouad's instructions were specific: load the passengers into lifeboats and scuttle the ship. One of the world's largest, most expensive cruise ships was to sink off the coast of Alexandria, with al Jazeera filming the event. Surely that would garner the world's attention.

The frightened passengers were to be guided safely ashore in Egypt, living proof of the terrorists' relative human compassion as the world was reminded of the Palestinians' dissatisfaction with their treatment by staid diplomats in their important institutes, conferences, and White Papers.

Palestinians like Fouad were weary of business as usual . . . with unconvincing crocodile tears shed as self-important players brokered 'peace' in so-called two-state solutions that never came to fruition. He tired of the world's stereotype of Arabs as a poorly educated bunch of disenfranchised's. If only the world's power elite -- the men who would provide the answers -- would refrain from offering empty promises and two-faced answers . . .

But in the best-laid plans, something always goes wrong. One of the men was unable to stick to the script. Couldn't resist seizing a prize trophy. The Star of David gold necklace was his prize, something he could carry back to the den, clenched between his teeth like a Kalahari tiger showing off his kill. He proudly brought it to the meeting with Fouad. As his leader entered the living room, he withdrew the necklace from his pocket. Belatedly, the man noticed something else -- a second necklace was entwined with his offering.

Surprise. Fear. How to explain this?! He recognized the second charm, a gold medallion of finely crafted filigreed oranges, with distinctive Arabic lettering on the back reading *"Hadera Citrus, Ltd."* He recognized it because he and others close to al Najimi, were given the same necklaces. There was the ever-present bowl of oranges on their boss's desk and the large, framed photograph of an old man standing in an orange grove, presumably taken in Hadera, Old Palestine. Fouad's fixation on oranges represented his loss, the reason for his passion. His men understood this.

But the hapless man discovered his mistake too late. His open palm was already extended. He quickly stepped to an open window with the charm. Fouad demanded the treasure. As Fouad slowly turned the charm over and over, no one dared speak. How could they have known such a token would be found around the neck of some American woman on board a cruise ship? The men entered the room triumphant. But the mood was no longer one of success. Quite the opposite. They held their collective breath as Fouad turned the charms over in his hand.

He stepped to the window, turning his back to them. Then he took a framed photograph from his desk. Slowly he removed the glass front. Then the cardboard backing. He withdrew an old photograph that had been hidden behind another one. It showed a young, happy woman, standing by a palm tree. Black curls framed a small oval face, her smile was jubilant. In her hands, she held the reins to a camel.

"Was this the woman?"

The man cowered now. He looked to his comrades for help. None was offered.

Louder now. "Was this the woman?!"

Silence filled the room.

"Get out." Fouad's voice was so low, his men could scarcely hear him.

Again. This time louder. "Get out!"

19

How does a man become a terrorist? Are the developmental stages the same as for a 'garden-variety' criminal? Once one peels back the terrorist rhetoric after all, aren't all bad guys, regardless of motivation, still bad guys? Common criminals? Perhaps, not harming for personal gain, but harming nevertheless? Taking from innocents. ˙Using violence. Breaking man's civic laws. Creating widows and orphans.

Some, unlike Fouad, were sociopaths, lacking any sense of decency, or of right or wrong. Those unfortunate enough to have met them could attest to their 'dead eyes.' With emotionless faces, these psychos offered no evidence of soul. There was no light, no life, no hope, no warmth. There was no order to their lives. They were so far removed from any connection to what is good and true, it was doubtful they could ever make it back to polite society, if indeed they'd ever dwelt there in the first place.

Fouad learned the hard way that some of these men were in his employ. Skilled in weapons and with radical beliefs, they were never more to him than hired mercenaries. Until their taking of the ship and Rachel's life, Fouad had not given much thought to other men's souls. Now, however, he spent more time in church, on his knees. He asked for God's forgiveness. He wondered if he could continue after this fierce event. Still intent on avenging his grandfather's life, Fouad had no further use for these men, whom he'd borrowed from the army of radicals he found hanging around the fringes of Cairo.

But for his men, it was a different story. They needed Fouad. They let a few weeks pass for him to cool off after their firings and were again standing at his front door.

"Al Najimi, we have to talk."

As they entered his ornate living room, Fouad was reminded he wanted nothing more to do with them. He noticed something about the men he somehow missed earlier: the men's obvious unease in his home. He watched as they glanced nervously at the oil paintings.

One man unceremoniously picked up an ornate cigarette case from a side table and peered inside. They were a rough bunch of men. Why was he just now seeing them in this light?

They began.

"Al Najimi. We know she was your friend. We get that. But time has passed. Have you given up now? Are you leaving us for good?"

Fouad didn't recall the man's name, nor did he wish to recall it. All he needed to know was standing before him. The man was of the desert. The desert fostered a certain strength in men. But underneath these country men there was also hatred. He could recognize this hatred because it seethed just beneath the surface in himself.

"Leader. It was her time. She died for our cause. It was Allah's will."

Fouad thought the man was a poster child for what many in the West believed about Islam and its practitioners. Militant. Loud. Opposite to so many in his homeland. Opposite to many good men who would seek justice. Fouad worked hard to remain neutral. He knew that making these men his enemy would help no one. And there was something else. They were his mirror now. A mirror he wished not to stare in for long.

Always pragmatic, his words did not reflect his emotions. Those were submerged. Those were private, known only to him. Instead, Fouad addressed them steadily and with a firm gaze, "I appreciate your words. Please, as we have discussed, I can no longer be your leader. I appreciate your understanding of my situation. Of course, our dilemma has not improved internationally. And certainly, as an attorney dealing in such matters, I shall continue to represent those needing my assistance."

The man's tone turned into anger. "Al Najimi, you need to continue as before. You need to stand outside the law. The law is what has brought us to this point. You must re-join us now."

Beyond Fouad's desire to disassociate himself from these men, there was something else informing his actions. The attorney in him dictated that he had no intention of sharing his plans with these militants. The last thing he needed now was a gang of operatives, liable to go off sending his mission backward. He'd learned his lesson. Too many men meant secrets shared. Secrets shared often resulted in missions being scrubbed. He would not kill again. But he did have a plan. A plan even his beautiful Aisha would not know.

"Ma'aleesh. I wish you all well. I am still in mourning. I hope that you can understand my position. The answer, gentlemen, must again be no. I cannot continue with you at this time. Perhaps sometime in the future . . . Please, I have a meal prepared for us. Come with me into the dining room. It will be my pleasure to serve you in my home."

With those kind words, Fouad defused the situation. And kept his own council. But Palestine continued to weigh on his mind. He kept a close watch on many of his fellow Palestinian refugees living in Cairo. While he regularly attended Mass at the Catholic church in Ma'adi, and had turned down the terrorists' invitation, Fouad was not exactly retired. He remained perched on a no-win fulcrum. For him, the contrast was stark and appalling: on one side, a potentially evil path, and on the other, a memory of a grandfather's dusty expectations.

As Rachel's murder propelled him back into darkness, he was aware of his grandfather's counsel night and day. He knew the old man was watching. The old man's kindly ghost chided him, encouraged him, and still helped him decide matters of importance.

The elder al Najimi was at the heart of Fou Fou's most vexing problems. While a world of guns and tough guys was not the old man's style, neither was a life of ease and separation from the Palestinian condition. In this, the grandson took a middle course. He refused to shun elegant drawing rooms for the austere existence of blood oaths. Despite the taking of the ship and his plan for new, more closely managed mayhem, he was convinced that matters of land ownership and sovereignty were best settled at the table of reason.

Getting everyone to that table . . . that was Fouad's dilemma. He needed to find a third way: Not accommodation. Not war. But a convincing bag of tricks to convince the West to deal seriously with him and his countrymen. If reason would not bring them to the table, fear would have to do. This was his unfortunate conclusion.

The Ivy League man as terrorist . . . "Some men rob you with a six gun; others rob you with a fountain pen." Fouad wanted ink, documents, land deeds, orange groves restored. No blood. The third way would paint a hologram of destruction. But it needed to be an infinitely believable hologram . . . of terror and consequences. Enough to bring those diplomat bastards to the bargaining table.

Fouad was far from a bin Laden for several reasons. The Saudi son came from great wealth but sought vengeance by renouncing the finer things of a materialistic world. He fought infidels in a far-off, third world country, secreted in the cold caves of a forbidding north. He was a tough man in exile from modern civilization and all it had to offer.

The man raised in the extreme poverty and discomfort of Palestine's dusty refugee camps, on the other hand, headed in an entirely different direction. By day, Fouad was a respected international attorney working for a prestigious New York law firm. As an adult, he was fond of old -world architecture, Oriental rugs, fine wines. He relied on trusted friends, worthy lovers. And more.

Once his mission was accomplished, he hoped for a sedate life of family, children, gourmet dinners, ski slopes, Wimbledon.

Unlike others who would commit terrorism, Fouad was strategic in his thinking. But Fouad, a man partly of the West, saw no need for the rigid confines of the Surah's of Islam. He remained content within the shelter of his Catholic faith.   He took communion. He delivered his confession in the booth only slightly less truthfully than other members of the flock. Surely, God had not yet abandoned Fouad. The Pope would understand.

"Bless him father, for he has sinned."

Fouad made his promise to himself and God in the Cairo Catholic parish he regularly visited: going forward, no one else would be harmed.

'Insha'allah.'

("God willing, and the creeks don't rise.")

20

"I stood again near it (the encampment of the tribe of Awfa) after an absence of twenty years, and with some efforts I know her abode again after thinking awhile."
"Refuge from Danger," by Zuhair (desert poet)

Fouad's discreet lifestyle began when he became a gentleman attorney of international law in an important New York law firm. Now, in Cairo's Garden City, an elegant antique-filled home provided him a safety and ease not available to most Palestinians. Fouad lived in a neighborhood of stately shade trees, fine, historic embassies, and the peace and quiet wealth affords to those similarly blessed the world over. Investments from his earlier, more materialistic, years spent as trade attorney funded his current lifestyle.

Cairo's power structure was well aware of the

gentleman lawyer/terrorist in its midst but turned a deaf ear to those who would bring him to international justice. Even as Egyptian officials winked at the West, drank cocktails with them at this party or that, they still harbored their own. It was the age-old law of the nomadic desert. Take care of those in your midst. This they did very, very well.

Covert strategy and a subconscious need to be closer to his grandfather led Fouad to establish his operations headquarters out in the desert, several miles beyond tourists and the Great Pyramid of Giza. Occasionally, Arabian horses carrying their riders galloped past the high-walled refuge cabin, but other than that, the location was private, remote and reminiscent of earlier times . . . of Lawrence of Arabia . . . of nomadic tribes . . . of the wonderful poetry of the desert . . .

There was no electricity there. Only lanterns to be lit at sunset. Sometimes, the Princeton man, the lawyer, the refugee, the lover, the guilty grandson, would come here to sit and breathe in the silence of the desert. Bedouin poetry was his constant companion, providing a measure of familiarity and solace.

The desert poet Zuhair's words spoken to him, calmed him, helped him sort things out . . . his deeds past and present, but particularly, his decisions for the future. At his core, he was still only a Palestinian refugee, wondering about his proper role in life. In need of certainty. Trouble is, there is no such thing as certainty in life for anyone, Palestinian or no.

Does the blackened ruin, situated in the stony ground
between Durraj and Mutathallam, which did not speak to me
when addressed, belong to the abode of Ummi Awfa?

And is it her dwelling at the two stony meadows, seeming
as though they were the renewed tattoo marks in the sinews of the wrist?

The wild cows and the white deer are wandering about
there, one herd behind the other, while their young are springing up
from every lying-down place.

I stood again near it (the encampment of the tribe of

Awfa) after an absence of twenty years, and with
some efforts
I know her abode again after thinking awhile.

I recognized the three stones blackened by fire at
the
place where the kettle used to be placed at night,
and the
trench round the encampment, which had not
burst, like the source of a pool.

And when I recognized the encampment I said to
its site,
'Now good morning, O spot!
May you be safe from dangers.'

Fouad carefully turned the tattered pages of the
book. He ran his fingers along the book's worn binding,
gazed at the clear desert full moon. Suddenly he missed
his woman. He needed to see her. Matters of the flesh
temporarily took precedence over any debt to an old man.

21

A call from one of Rossie's stateside friends triggered a sudden sense of homesickness.

"Rossberg, You old reprobate. Have we lost you to the sands of the desert forever? When are you coming home?"

Rossie was happy to hear his old friend's voice. A voice with the familiar New York ring to it. A friend and a culture he missed.

"Just some last business I'm finishing up. You understand, related to Rachel."

"We heard you were a spy. Is that true?"

Rossie laughed. "Hardly. No, my friend, as I told you, Rachel and I have spent many years here in this part of the world. I'm just . . . you know . . . "

The words wouldn't come to him. His friend, sensing his distress backed off to their usual humor to relieve the moment.

"You know, you still owe me from that last poker game. And I'm holding you to it. Unless, of course, when you return we have a rematch."

The two continued talking. They caught up on most of their news. Rossie, as usual, could not confirm nor deny . . .but it was good to hear a friendly voice from New York.

After the call, Rossie poured himself a glass of wine and settled in for the evening. Fouad wasn't the only man who sought solace in the wisdom of the Bedouin. Rossie, too, connected with desert poets, authentic scribes of the Near East's distant past. Communing with the desert wisdom of Sufi poets helped place Rossie's current life into perspective. That was one great thing about being a scholar by profession: he could easily slip into the back recesses of his own mind. He could read, research, contemplate, escape. Add a few glasses of wine, and the tug of uncontrollable grief could be temporarily kept at bay.

He selected as his company those of greater wisdom. Sometimes that wisdom came to him through the Torah. Other times, it was provided by desert nomads of the past. He needed no pass to meet these thinkers. Only a pair of scratched horned rim glasses. Rossie assumed his usual seat perched between reality and fantasy. He wondered, was it all fantasy? Had he already died?

In his reveries he felt Rachel with him, but not as she was when he last saw her. For some reason, the Rossie of late found himself traveling all the way back to the beginning. To the pretty Jewish princess, he first took to a favorite Italian restaurant in Hell's Kitchen. The unfinished dinner as they first gazed into each other's eyes. The passion of finally finding 'The One.'

Who was Antar? Some poet. How could he know Rossie's young mind so well?

When she captivates you with a mouth possessing
sharp and white teeth,
sweet as to its place of kissing, delicious of taste.

As if she sees with the two eyes of a young, grown-
up gazelle from the deer.
It was as though the musk bag of a merchant in his
case of perfumes
preceded her teeth toward you from her mouth.

Or as if it is an old wine-skin, from Azri'at,
preserved long,
such as the kings of Rome preserve.

Rossie read the poem as he sipped a Cypriot wine
seated on the deck of his new houseboat. With these
gentle thoughts, he felt a new sense of ease. Perhaps a
normal man would let his love remain in his heart awhile
longer. . .

Or her mouth is as an un-grazed meadow,
whose herbage the rain has guaranteed,
in which there is but little dung;
and which is not marked with the feet of animals.

. . . or perhaps a sane man would accept his life and his
own wife's death with more grace. Perhaps revenge was a
bad idea.

Rossie recalled an old proverb: **"Two eyes for an eye."**

He waited, drink in hand. With a stunning view of the distant pyramids rising above one of his favorite cities. But for his mission, it was a magical time. The stranger who stole his peaceful life would show up eventually and then maybe he would shoot him. He had no idea how it would happen. But he vowed to look him in the eye and personally deliver Rachel's revenge and his own demand for payback.

Eventually he returned inside to refresh his drink. And to locate and reload his revolver. A stun gun rested in the drawer near his revolver. The thought occurred to him that the stun gun – friend of little old ladies and neighborhood watch cops – might prove to be his weapon of choice when the time came.

Rossie poured a double shot of gin, the better to view the last moments of a Cairo evening.

22

"There is family business, Melvin."

His brother's tone had a note of seriousness. Conscious of the many analysts monitoring the call, Melvin spoke in his usual riddles. "The estate again?"

Alberto, aware of their prearranged code, responded in kind.

"Yes. There are some papers you need to sign. What if we got together, say in Paris? I'm attending a scientific conference there next month." Melvin knew Alberto's call had nothing to do with any estate. Plans were made. They would meet in two weeks. Alberto would stay with Judith at their new retirement apartment.

Melvin's days with the government were now numbered, drawing down to a life of ease. Even from his powerful vantage point, Melvin was growing tired of tracking 30,000 European and Northern American expatriates living in Egypt. Most of his charges were based in the capital city of Cairo, although growing numbers of expats worked in Luxor, Alexandria or the Red and Mediterranean Sea resorts. All were greeted upon arrival at Cairo's main airport by uniformed member of Egypt's national forces, combat clad, loaded rifles at the ready. Less obvious to newcomers was Melvin lurking in the background.

It's possible to split the majority of expatriates living in Egypt into two groups. Some, like Rossie, are "employed" before expatriating. Others often take jobs and work within the local Egyptian economy and earn their wages in Egyptian pounds or *guinayh*. One internet tourist web site urges potential residents not to be afraid of the chaotic, exciting, fast pace of life. "Be prepared to socialize until all hours of the night and ignore much of the media's portrayal of Egypt because it is in fact a very safe place to live apart from the odd bit of pick-pocketing that goes on in the most popular tourist haunts."

What the tourist pamphlets fail to mention, however, is the fact that one's name is processed upon arrival, and one's whereabouts are tracked by Egyptian authorities. Careful identification is made for all residents. And if one knows Melvin? 'Processing' of certain individuals can be a tad more strenuous. One can count on GPS tracking devices on cars, listening bugs in one's apartment, and facial recognition photos on file. In short, wherever you are, if you know Melvin or even if you don't, he might be listening. You will always have a friend in Melvin.

One might call Melvin a contented man. After years of toiling in one government bureaucracy after another, he was now finishing his estimable career in a position of power. While no one arrived in Egypt without Melvin's knowledge, his known affiliation with the C.I.A. afforded him a sort of respect that bordered on fear. Even American ambassadors gave the man a wide berth. No one wanted to cross him. Because, like all good civil servants the world over, Melvin knew where the proverbial bodies were buried. One might add, '. . . having buried many of them himself . . .'

He could render advice as to who might be rewarded with a term spent in the rough hands of Egyptian 'justice.' With an imperceptible nod of his world-weary head, he could effect a person's transfer to Egyptian authorities for certain 'procedures.' Such procedures ran the gamut from simple incarceration to ones involving electric wires, urine-soaked terrors and other unsavory acts not offered by America's more genteel holding facilities.

Indeed, as most fortunate's sipped their gins and tonics at the Gezira Club positioned on an island in the middle of the Nile, others begged for water in less than posh surroundings somewhere north, in the Nile Delta. And Melvin could be the cause. Visitors to Egypt freely enjoyed its ancient ruins, oblivious to the less fortunate fate of some. So much as a heavy sigh from Melvin delivered to the right Egyptian official, and a person might 'disappear.' Those ex-pats who lived in Egypt beyond the three-month mark, however, became aware of this man's power. Everyone wanted Melvin to be happy. It is always better to feed the lizard on a regular schedule.

And what of such a man's motivations? Do the math. A life spent on a relatively limited civil service salary. A life spent watching millionaires and billionaires frolicking in the sun. A life of increasing power. A life few could control near the end. He was, after all, a trusted civil servant. His track record was exemplary. Always the company man. Always doing the right thing. A man on whom America could depend.

As retirement loomed, would Melvin settle for the little house somewhere in America? Would he be content simply to recall the luxuries he had experienced overseas? The servants cleaning his homes? The waiters passing him his drink and snack? The chauffeur driven cars?

Of course not.

And now, it was time for Melvin's master plan to commence. There were certain State secrets that might be sold for a price. There was one particularly large item that would guarantee Melvin his Parisian town home and those annual 'vacances' in 'Sud de France.' That's where Alberto came in. The wheels were in motion. Soon the trade would be possible, and a discreet Swiss bank account would be filled with *shekels* to bankroll Melvin's 'declining years.' This senior citizen would be padded, comforted, massaged, and well satisfied with his lot in life.

"Judith. I'm glad I caught you in. So, you have signed the lease today?"

"Yes, dear. The apartment is a bit shabby, if you ask me. Our laundry is located on another floor, and we must share it with other tenants! Are you sure this is what you want?"

"It's a beginning. Let us settle first. Let me complete my retirement business. Then, as I told you before, we shall see what other arrangements might be made later."

Almost as an after-thought, "By the way, Alberto will be arriving in Paris in a coupl'a weeks. I told him we'd put him up. Make sure there's an extra bed. I might stop in as well."

Judith wasn't surprised by this last-minute remark. She was used to a husband for whom secrecy and a life spent on the run were normal. Melvin was just being Melvin. Again.

Her husband was on the march. And the chances were better than even that his final landing spot would not be shabby. Not for this man of the world. A global citizen. Gone would be Spaghetti-O's. In their place? Fine French wines. Pates. Local charcuteries. Nothing but the best for a faithful civil servant, about to enjoy his golden years, with a dutiful wife used to not asking too many questions.

Karen Hagestad Cacy

23

" . . And verily, as to the folly of an old man,
there is no wisdom after it,
but the young man after his folly may become
wise . . ."
"Refuge from Danger," by Zuhair (desert poet)

Rossie was well aware he had his own special listening world hanging on his every phone conversation. But in his new, more laid-back lifestyle, he had nothing to hide. 'Knock yourself out, Melvin,' was his thought. He was more than a little tired of cops and robbers, strange men warning him off, and his own growing paranoia. He suspected Werner, for instance, of something. Of what, he was not quite certain. But the man gave off a certain aura of strangeness.

To shake himself back to a new normal, Rossie settled into a sedate daily schedule. He woke up late and made his way to Groppi's for a cup of Arabic coffee. From there, he strolled back to the Nile for a proper breakfast in the coffee shop of the Shepheard's Hotel. The balance of his day was spent reading, writing, napping, and in the avoidance therapy most people the world over practiced over ice.

Several weeks in on his new regimen, and it was working beautifully. He was now sleeping through the night, lulled to sleep by the slight movement of the houseboat in the water. He began fixing up his place, with bowls of fresh fruit, flowers, and the comforting hum of classical music in the background. Without being consciously aware of it, he was busily reinventing his Stateside home, the one he shared with Rachel just two years earlier. Shoved to the back of his mind, always were the distinct facts that this was not New York, Rachel was nowhere about, and his domesticity was nothing more than an act . . . life imitating life . . . but an earlier, happier life.

And on a weekday like any other, as clockwork, he opened his copy of the International Tribune at his usual round marble topped table in Groppi's. The fresh, strong coffee was very hot, and so he turned to his first pursuit of the day, a reprint of the New York Times crossword puzzle. The coffee cup teetered unsteadily in its saucer, spilling hot coffee on his paper. As Rossie lifted the cup to his mouth, he saw the reason: There, coiled neatly inside the saucer's grooved center, were Rachel's two gold charm necklaces. She wore them always, even while bathing. One necklace featured the Star of David, and the other bore a replica of an orange.

Rossie had always puzzled over the Arabic writing on the orange necklace. She never revealed its meaning to him. "Hadera Citrus, Ltd." Hadera, Rossie knew, was a small beach town in Israel. Perhaps there was no meaning, had been his conclusion. Just something she picked up when she was working in Israel, a pretty trinket. Something told him to leave it at that. Today, however, its message raised disturbing questions.

A waiter approached him as he refilled his coffee. "Sayid Rossberg, please take care. The fresh coffee is very hot today. Please do not burn yourself."

The man had never before approached him at his table. Coffee is hot. It's always hot. Why warn him? Clearly, someone was continuing the game. Now he knew there'd be more to follow. Rossie picked up the necklace, held it tight for a small prayer, then placed it carefully away in his shirt pocket. Perhaps he would visit the shooting range after breakfast.

24

"Habibi."

"Aywah."

The satellite picked up the phone call from a burn phone. Later it would be translated into Hebrew. The Arabic-speaking callers were expressing their anger at one Fouad al Najimi. According to the rant, al Najimi was a quitter, no longer deserving of their loyalty or trust. Besides, continued the callers, citing damning evidence, the man was schooled in America. His woman was an American impersonating an Arab. The worst rap on him, though, was his wealth. A successful attorney with art on his walls. How did a refugee advance that high? Where was al Najmi's true allegiance, they wondered.

The Americans and Egyptians weren't the only ones tracking who came, went and lingered in Cairo. Josh in Tel Aviv and Isaiah, originally from Israel's coastal town of Petah-Tiqwa, also counted noses. In Cairo, as in other world capitals, Israeli Mossad was present . . . in mosques, behind hotel potted palms, even camped out near money changers' back-alley shops.

Isaiah and his friends also lurked around Cairo's Coptic Christian and Roman Catholic churches, and the lone synagogue in the Ma'adi district. Going about their business, Isaiah's team was discrete, technically equipped with the latest in paraphernalia, and keeping their own counsel.

Today, Tel Aviv's 'Man-in-Cairo' was early for his meeting. Rather than see his contact in a downtown location, Isaiah chose a crowded spot, a place where everyone was self-absorbed, busily moving from here to there in Cairo's international airport coffee shop. A group of Chinese tourists sat at a nearby table, jabbering in Chinese. The waiter barely noticed him and anyway was too busy to give a damn if he did.

Isaiah's contact approached. Isaiah found it difficult to suppress a laugh.

"Ah, my little 'schnitzel.' Shalom."

When he answered Isaiah, 'Schnitzel's' voice was deep and masculine, a mismatch to his effeminate appearance and mincing steps as he approached the table.

"Knock it off, Isaiah."

"A purse, 'Werner?' A purse?!"

"I said knock it off."

But Isaiah couldn't help himself. His friend looked so ridiculous. Totally believable, but ridiculous.

"Is this what they did to you?"

He referred to Mossad's excellent wardrobe and prop boys. Closely linked to Israel's stage and film industry, the agency was one of the best outfitters in the clandestine world.

"Are you done yet?"

"Yes. Of course. But, really, 'Werner,' you are a picture. Wait until I tell Miriam."

"Uh-uh-uh. Company discretion, old boy. Can we begin?"

Isaiah winked at his friend.

"Just put your purse out of sight, sweetie. And tell me about your newest tenant."

"His aim is improving."

Isaiah nodded. "Visits to the shooting range."

"Melvin has him on the down low at present. I'm sure our friendly CIA is up to something. Otherwise, Mr. Rossberg would have left town by now. After all, as we know the professor has a son and a tenured position awaiting him stateside. Why stay? He must still be on the payroll."

Isaiah issued Werner further instructions. "Hmm. Josh wants us to step up surveillance of Fouad al Najimi. You know who he is. Wealthy attorney here in town.

Lives in Garden City. Sharia Kasr el Aini. Particularly watch his connections to others."

"Isaiah, where do you want me? I can't be everywhere, you know. You guys need to make up your minds."

"Look, Werner, I'll cover al Najimi for you, if you'll keep tabs on Melvin and Rossberg. All three are up to something, if you ask me. Josh's famous intuition at work again."

"He's not often wrong."

"Another thing: Josh has a little trip in mind for our scholar. In the meantime, though, you're doing great. Josh is still worried about Rossberg's mental state since his wife's killing. Anything to report there?"

"He's on a more relaxed schedule. A bit of alcohol at sunset. Okay. More than a little. Other than that, he seems to be coming along."

"Very well then. Good work – carry on, old boy.
Look, I'm late for my meeting with Melvin. Here, my
little 'schnitzel.' You can finish my pastry."

"I'd better, old boy. Looks as if you could stand to
lose a few pounds . . ."

'Werner's' final words were delivered to thin air.
Isaiah already was gone. He knew how to disappear. He
had just demonstrated the skill. 'Schnitzel,' reached for
his purse, returning in an instant to his odd Swiss persona.
The better to watch what Mossad paid him to watch.

Isaiah left his meeting east of downtown and
proceeded to a small café in Giza on the city's western edge.
The carefully selected shabby falafel shop frequented by
locals worked well for both men. Besides ethnicity, Isaiah
shared something else with Kenneth L. Rossberg, Sr. – a
distinct dislike of Melvin. Mossad was well aware of the
complexities of their American contact. They paid as much
attention to Melvin some weeks as they did to known al
Qaeda operatives in Egypt. On Isaiah's agenda today was
Fouad al Najimi. Was he a member of al Qaeda? A loner?
Retired? He wanted to find out what Melvin knew. It

would be the usual cat and mouse number. Getting information out of Melvin was always difficult at best.

On his way to the café, Isaiah checked in with Josh in Tel Aviv, who fed him a few harmless tidbits to share with their American 'colleague.' As Isaiah entered the lean-to shop near the desert's edge, he immediately spotted Melvin, seated in a corner, wearing a khaki safari hat pulled low over his face, chowing down on a sandwich. Some of its contents had escaped the wrap onto the tabletop. Isaiah could never figure out if Melvin really was a slob, or if it was some sort of cover, designed to derail any notion of him as the Free World's 'lead dog' in Egypt.

Melvin, with whom Mossad professed to work closely, was not a friend. The boys from Tel Aviv had his number from the start. With Melvin, as with their other adversaries, they were on constant alert. They had him on tape. They kept amazingly current with Melvin's work.

"Marhaba. Marhaba." Melvin greeted Isaiah in the standard Arabic greeting.

Squinting at Isaiah from beneath his hat brim, Melvin slowly wiped his mouth with his napkin, then carefully wiped the tabletop immediately in front of him. Isaiah noticed he stopped exactly at what would be the center line of the small table. The spilt food on Isaiah's side he carefully left untouched. After this ritual, Melvin began with a bang: "So, tell me, how are things with our mutual friend 'Werner' today?"

"Alright, Melvin."

"Funny costume though, that Swiss get-up."

"I'll give you that. But you know we have to watch. Speaking of which -- we notice your man is still in Cairo. Didn't you fire him? We're still collecting rent from him."

Melvin fired back sarcastically: "Israel doesn't get enough foreign aid. We want to supplement our contribution, you know . . . for 'the cause.' The U.S. Congress expects nothing less."

Touche.

The two sat and stared at each other for a while. Poker without the cards. Finally, the American blinked.

"Look, I'll level with you."

That'll be the day, thought Isaiah.

"Tell Josh, it's quite simple. Even transparent. Rossberg's a translator. Nothing more. The man's had a rough go. I know you are aware. Losing his wife and all. I was hoping to bring him along in due time. Teach him the ropes. Expand his duties here. Fact is, I've learned the hard way, he is inept. Drinking. Undependable. A few lies here and there. Hell, Fouad's men actually captured him a while ago."

"What?!"

"More like catch and release. I see you're surprised. I'm surprised you're surprised. Rossberg chose not to tell me about that little incident. If I can't trust someone, that's it. He's out! So, you see, Isaiah, we can let this one go. Take him. He is untrustworthy. And of course, he is a member of your tribe anyway."

There it was. The dig. Not unexpected. Not the first time. The Ugly American, the anti-Semite. The man of poor manners and worse social class. But Isaiah didn't care. Because the meeting just more than paid for itself: Isaiah knew Josh would enjoy hearing of Rossberg's silence. Maybe he could keep his mouth shut, this professor.

Melvin continued. "I would hope, however, that if 'Werner' does happen to pick anything up of mutual interest, you'll let me know. As per our agreement."

As if Melvin didn't already have his microphones positioned at all the keyholes. But they had to do this. There was pride and a certain deniability in the men's dance. Mossad listens. America listens. Everyone shares information. Yeh, right. Of course, they do.

At this, Melvin's voice trailed off, his meaning, clear. Mossad and the CIA, together forever. 'Kumbayah.' Sharing secrets.

Isaiah thought. Like we're going to trust you.

Isaiah broached his main subject. "Fouad al Najmii."

Melvin paused mid-bite. "What about him?"

"Know him?"

"Yes, I know him. International attorney. Schooled in America. A Palestinian. Bit of a chip on his shoulder. But, as with several others here in town, we keep track, naturally. I can tell you he's not a simple man. His hands have been in a few things in the past."

"The ship?"

"We can't prove that."

"The ship?" Isaiah wasn't backing down. Mossad already knew the truth. But he couldn't resist poking Melvin.

"Perhaps. Look, Isaiah. Let me tell you about al Najimi. Brilliant. Catholic. Wealthy. Has a steady, albeit much younger, American girl friend. I don't think he's necessarily anyone to worry about. Not now. Look, he has a life. He has no desire to die early. Perhaps the ship. We have no proof. We happen to believe the man's taking early retirement. From revenge, I mean."

Melvin wanted Mossad to back off al Najimi. That was another tidbit Isaiah picked up he knew Josh would find interesting. Based on what, Isaiah wondered. Their meeting continued. Isaiah shared Josh's news items with Melvin, noting the other's distinct interest. He seemed to accept their lukewarm offering of information. Isaiah finished off his greasy falafel and left. No sense pretending their snack was anything other than a lizards' convention. Two secret men slithering along the same wall until one either falls asleep or slips off.

Later, he debriefed Josh by secure phone. "Good work. Interesting reaction to al Najimi. Bears watching. Werner can stay in place for now. But be sure to let him know the Americans are along for the ride."

"Josh, it's pretty clear Melvin's cut Rossberg loose. The man lied to him. He has a point. What exactly do we think this Rossberg can do for us?"

"It may be more a case of what we can do for him. The story is complicated. Some of it for now is need to know. As it unravels, perhaps the man will take our side. Critical moments can arise quickly, as you know."

Isaiah was less than satisfied with Josh's explanation. But Josh was in charge of the operation. Isaiah was only eyes and ears on the ground. He surmised Rossberg's recruitment might be imminent. To prepare, he returned to his apartment and spent several hours poring over Mossad's file on the professor. He was certain he would need all the information he could gather. The file did not disappoint – it was thick with details.

An Arabic-speaking Jew well versed in the ways and byways of the Middle East was a man to be watched. America's recruitment of Rossie was not ill-informed. Over the years, Mossad also had Rossberg in their sights. They kept their eyes on the reclusive professor, busy at his work. Rossberg's transparency was well documented in his numerous articles, translations and books. His middle of the road stance on the Arab-Israeli conflict was well known. Another college professor professing his lack of bias, one way or the other.

Since Rachel's 'incident,' however, and Rossie's short-lived career with Melvin, Mossad's surveillance of him increased. They watched the professor carefully for any sea change in his neutrality; murder can do that even to a learned man. Their amplifiers were positioned beside Melvin's in the houseboat. Until they weren't. The Israelis decommissioned as much technology as they installed. Why share information? Melvin and the Mossad played their usual game of cat and mouse. Each could identify the other's distinctive wire cutter marks. Both recognized the Russians' marks – as usual, they used cheap shears. Some things never change.

Werner continued his work, a sort of house arrest so discrete, Rossie came and went unaware of his presence. If Mossad would trust anyone it would begin with a fellow Jew. Rossie would receive their invitation soon. Their files on Rossie and Fouad al Najimi grew thicker by the day. Now Melvin was trying to move them away from al Najmii. Why? What did Melvin know? Meanwhile, many man hours had gone into their Rossberg strategy. Mr. Hibbard wasn't included in their plans.

Surveillance on Melvin also increased. He was close to retirement. Would he go quietly, or would he do

damage on his way out the door? Melvin's character was
questionable. Now, time would tell whether Mossad's
psychological profile of 'Hibbard" was correct. One thing
they noted: the man's movements were becoming less
predictable. Would he cash out before leaving his final
posting in Cairo? Much of the information Melvin was
privy to over his long career could be tagged for sale on
the open market. They knew certain clients – the usual
suspects, and there were many -- would pay top dollar for
what Melvin could place on the selling block.

Josh and Isaiah installed new, state-of-the-art
directional microphones linked to a satellite to better
retrieve Melvin's conversations -- indoors, on the
sidewalk, even as he stood holding a drink in the middle
of the pool at the Gezira Club. They weren't privy to the
man's office calls. Those still were safely guarded by the
U.S.'s high-tech lead shielding hidden inside the falling
down excuse of a building that housed America's Egypt
desk.

Judith Hibbard, they learned, was soon to arrive
for a visit from her Parisian location. No doubt, the two
would be finalizing details of Melvin's impending

retirement. Werner became a regular fixture in the airport's coffee shop as Mossad awaited Judith's plane.

25

Cairo Customs had a last- minute personnel
change. Werner sat in the coffee shop, as Judith Hibbard's
BOAC Flight #123 from Paris arrived. "She's on this
flight. Here she comes. Check everything. Be careful."
The regular inspector welcomed the offer of a coffee
break.

His replacement addressed the American woman
at his counter. "Madam. Welcome to Egypt. I see you
are traveling alone today . . . and on diplomatic passport."

"Yes. Thank you. Usually, I pass through one of
the doors over there."

"'Usually' is no more, madam. Perhaps you've
heard, there is a war on terrorism underway. Even here, in
peaceful Egypt. Please step into the room with our female
attendant. This will not take long."

Judith was incensed. No one had treated her like this before. She was an important person, after all. At least her husband was. And by extension, so was she.

"I will need your jacket, shoes and carry-on, please." The attendant could not have been more courteous in her request.

Judith complied.

"What are these?" The attendant held up Judith's heavy set of decorating fabric samples linked together by a circular metal ring.

"Fabric samples. My husband asked me to bring them. I am decorating his den in our Paris apartment."

The inspector checked carefully. Finding nothing suspicious, she released Judith into a gaggle of tourists just cleared from an Alitalia flight from Rome. The woman clutched her carry-on, struggling to keep a grip on the heavy fabric samples as she made her way to baggage. She was slightly middle-aged plump, but had an open manner, a woman who normally smiled easily. She showed her passport to the last exit guard. Noting her diplomatic stamp, he directed her away from the crowd and ushered her through a special side gate. There, she thought, that's more like it.

Melvin's wife arrived on time and as instructed from Paris. With her was the signed lease on their new apartment; her fingers were stained red from the paint she already had applied to her husband's new library. Melvin insisted on his library. Matching leather chairs already were on order from a Norwegian supplier.

Her hand-carried sample stack of fabrics made it through the airport check points with nary a mention. They were what they were. What wife does not take fabric samples to her husband for final approval? What woman would not wish to know her husband's viewpoint on decorating his library? What woman would not appear more innocent than this short American woman in her matching sweater set?

Melvin greeted his wife warmly. "No, no. I know you are tired. Rest. Let me look at these. I believe I'll look at them outside."

With those welcoming words, Melvin left his wife with a cold lemonade to take her nap. He carried her heavy pile of fabric samples to his car and drove out to the pyramids. Isaiah watched Melvin's car as it arrived in Giza and turned onto a remote desert road.

The car's windows were wide open, and Melvin was listening to the BBC News station. He got out of the car with his fabric samples and sat on a bench. His movements were slow and uninteresting. He paused to open a Stella Beera. As he downed the cold drink, he squinted at the Sphinx seated in the distance in the hot sun.

He knew he was being watched. Have a good look, boys. Nothing to see here. An American Chief of Station enjoying an innocent afternoon in Giza. Right.

Two inscrutables: Melvin Hibbard and the Sphinx. The statue was missing her nose, thanks to Napoleon's soldiers, who shot it off many years earlier. Melvin's nose, so far, was intact. Slowly, he considered each sample, feeling its texture, turning it over and over in the bright sunlight.

What the hell. A boring man. No doubt hen-pecked in the bargain, Isaiah thought, as he watched Melvin through a high-powered lens. Melvin was putting his watcher to sleep. He knew that. However, hidden in the samples was one of America's most guarded and as yet unused, weapons systems. It appeared innocuous. It was not. The satellite coordinates and logarithmic formulas gave the user the capability to commandeer and redirect a satellite's mission.

Lives of ease soon would await Melvin and Judith. He carefully placed the important instructions inside the napkin he was using to catch the beer's moisture. That one action alone should have alerted Isaiah that something was amiss. Since when did Hibbard care about neatness? Instead, he watched as Melvin climbed back in his car and drove off. Unseen by Mossad, Melvin tossed the empty bottle and its napkin into the utility tray between the front seats. Somewhere en route back to Cairo, he moved the paper from the tray to a breast pocket. Clever man, Melvin. Enjoying a bottle of beer out by the pyramids. Time for his wife to have a nap. Chalas'na. It's done.

Fabric for his den draperies having been chosen,
Melvin drove back to town. He showed Judith his choice.
She was pleased at his selection.

"Is this it then?"

"Yes, Judith. You have done well, my dear. The
green velvet holds the light very well. I checked. Now let
me take you to the club. You must be hungry after your
journey."

26

"Werner. What are you doing here?"

Melvin greeted Werner at the Gezira Club's lounge by the pool, where he had taken Judith for dinner and drinks. His manner had all the warmth of an Egyptian asp.

"I'm a member, my good man. Isaiah sends you his best, by the way. And this must be the lovely Judith."

Judith extended her hand. Melvin quickly grabbed his wife's hand and unceremoniously pulled her to her feet.

"My wife just arrived. As you well know. Why are you fellas following me around? Run out of bad guys to chase? Maybe you didn't get the memo. We're supposed to be allies."

"Hey!" For a short moment the Swiss man dropped his demeanor to take offense. "Cairo's a small town. Don't flatter yourself -- just because we happen to see each other here or there. Maybe it has something to do with your retirement, old boy." Werner made sure he stressed the word old. "Perhaps you fear no one will care what you do after a while. You imagine everyone you come across is interested in you. Methinks, pure psychology."

At this insult, Melvin abruptly grabbed their drinks and steered Judith towards the dining room. Who was Werner anyway? Just some low level pissant who reported to Isaiah. He made a mental note to complain to Josh later about him. Not that it would do any good. Those Israeli's stuck together.

"Touchy, old man!" Werner called out to Melvin's departing back as he took a seat by the pool. A waiter brought him his refill. He enjoyed mocking Melvin. He thought he might do it again and more often. No one said he had to be nice to Melvin. That was Isaiah's job. Werner would have his fun.

Most of Cairo's international set seemed to be at the club that night. Even Rossie, who caught Werner and Melvin's odd exchange from his post seated at a table behind a potted palm. Interesting that Melvin and Werner were acquainted. Now he knew. Werner, his rather strange landlord wasn't Swiss. Nor was he American. What else was there? Israeli. His landlord was Mossad.

He could feel his legs weakening. Every time he gained secure footing, something else happened to remove it. Bad enough that he was sitting around all day waiting for some faceless Arab terrorist to visit so he could kill him. Rossie felt a noose tightening around his own neck. When he arrived in Cairo, he was Melvin's bait, dangled at will around Cairo. Now free to go back to Kenneth and his sedate academic life, instead he chose to bait his own hook. It was becoming clear that as he drew closer to the killer, he was going to have company . . . America . . . Israel . . . probably Russia . . . come one, come all.

Rossie decided to refrain from approaching either man. Why feign camaraderie? Two of the last people he wished to see tonight, or any night. Where was the trust? Rossie decided on steak for dinner.

Despite its reputation, Mossad occasionally missed things . . . discoveries . . . clever weapons systems. Melvin, they thought, was an easy read. They knew he was up to things. The man was slippery. But all they had so far were his preparations to leave Cairo. They noted Judith's recent sightseeing excursion to Zurich. There, she checked the couple's safety deposit box in a bank of inestimable reputation. No one noticed the paper she placed in her blouse before exiting the bank. No one witnessed her transfer the paper to the cardboard backing of her fabric samples. Not even Mossad. Everyone can't see everything all the time.

Meanwhile, Tel Aviv's planning team remained in the background, on call at a moment's notice to analyze events, strangers, operatives, crises. Josh's growing agenda was filled with names, suspicions, bits of seemingly unrelated data. One thing he knew for certain, the current cocktail of individuals wandering the streets of Cairo could spell trouble. He wished to know why Melvin was intent on diverting them away from al Najimi. With these thoughts in mind, Josh was about to add Rossie to 'Team Israel.'

There was a lot Rossie had yet to learn about those who would guard his people's homeland. Jews with microphones and computer experts would be filling him in eventually.

But not yet. Tonight, he ordered the steak.

27

'Shui lo shih chu.' – As the water recedes, the rock appears.
Old Chinese proverb

Ken worked for a mid-range law firm in Mid-Town. His paycheck was still on the low side, barely enough for him to afford a studio apartment in a gentrified area of Harlem. His firm handled primarily corporate law. Most of his cases were enough to put a person to sleep. Balance sheets, investor relations, quarterly reports, transparency, federal tax law. Hardly edgy subjects.

Occasionally, he'd accompany senior partners as potential clients were interviewed. Such meetings often took place in wood-paneled boardrooms at some higher-level suite overlooking the city. Coffee usually was served with small pastries in the swanker law firms.

At one such meeting, no one noticed the server who passed the refreshments, refilled coffee carafes, and disposed of dirty cups and plates. The man was especially careful with Ken's cup. His gloved fingers carefully carried the cup to the back kitchen, where it was placed into an evidence bag. The bag was transported by taxi to an innocuous row house several blocks away.

The brownstone bore no street number. There was a state -of- the- art security camera filming the stoop. And there was a grate into which potential visitors might speak to a disembodied voice somewhere inside. Some who entered, did so with a code phrase, changed on a regular basis. Today's code was "Star of David."

Visitors who gained entry were buzzed into a foyer with steel doors and another camera. The procedure continued through two more layers until an actual human secretary greeted the visitor to escort them upstairs.

This was Mossad's New York City operations center. Naturally, the Soviets, Chinese and Americans all knew exactly who the building housed. Still there was the ritual secrecy. Inside, special walls and the latest in technology worked well to keep safe the Israeli's daily business.

As for those housed there: Physically, they were a curious bunch of spies. Each was over six feet, fair skinned, with blonde hair, and looked like he could stop a Mack truck with one arm. The men more closely resembled Swiss army guards, German wrestlers, or even members of America's elite Seal Team Six. Walking around Mid-town, no one would guess that these men were some of Israel's finest.

Ken's coffee cup was directed to their lab. There, an expert extracted the needed information – fingerprints and DNA – information that was transmitted back to the team in Tel Aviv for their work. Ken Rossberg was to be part of the Master Plan. But first, they needed to confirm his identity. And so, this information was added to the file. For use later. It confirmed what they already knew.

It's good to check.

172

28

The alcohol wasn't working.

Rossie suddenly felt old and frail. The first time it happened was on his morning walk through Garden City. There was a cool breeze, the heat of the city had yet to take hold. He interrupted his stroll to perch on a stone wall outside the American Embassy. Two Marine guards regarded him carefully. What they saw was an American Jew. An old man. A sad person. Nothing to see here. Move along, folks.

Rossie was no longer sure of who he was. He had no business living in Cairo. His Rachel was still gone. What was changed by his actions? His son needed him. His Bedouin desert poetry was failing him. Of what value are intellectual pursuits if a man's spirit is dead? And what if his legs can no longer hold him? Where was his life? Perhaps it was over, and he was just now realizing it.

Rossie rose to leave. He felt the sudden need to be home in his houseboat, surrounded again by familiar things. His legs crumpled beneath him. The guards raced to help. Later he recalled being helped inside the embassy. Being given a brief medical check- up. Being driven home. He remembered a nattily dressed Marine walking him inside, making sure he was all right. Of particular note, Rossie remembered the look on Werner's face as he peered around the corner – commotion and gossip always were so interesting to this disturbing little man. As he now suspected, Israel's man-in-Cairo, on patrol.

Rossie trusted no one. Including himself. He poured another drink. And waited for Rachel's killer to appear.

29

The man in question was busily lighting candles in Garden City. Chilling champagne. Greeting the caterer delivering an exquisite four-course dinner. Fou Fou was expecting his woman to join him for dinner. His grandfather probably would not approve of the massive diamond ring in his pocket. He hated conspicuous consumption. But Aisha was a woman to keep for life. She deserved nothing less.

"Fou Fou, the New York Knicks won!" This was her greeting as she threw open his front door. The two shared a passion for U.S. basketball, especially for their 'hometown' New York team.

Fouad always could count on Aisha to bring a bubbling joy into his home. He could no more do without her laughter than without air. Hers was the first voice he wished to hear on waking and the last he wished to hear before falling to sleep. The scent of her skin was enough to settle him down. He buried his face in her neck and breathed in his woman's jasmine scent. A small gray box held the huge diamond engagement ring circled with her favorite gem, twenty sapphires, Fouad purchased on a recent business trip to Dubai. Her slender dancer's hand would be the perfect background for such luxury.

"Aisha, we are dining formally this evening."

He ushered a surprised Aisha into the low-lit dining room. The crystal goblets and fine China were a change from their usual dinners in.

"Fou Fou. What is all of this?"

As if she did not know. The girl had been waiting for her man to commit in such a romantic way for a long time. Obviously, tonight was the night. Her eyes glistened with tears of happiness. Fouad approached her and fell to his knees.

"Sweet Aisha. You are my life. I cannot live without you by my side. My Anne. I love you forever. Please, will you be my wife? Will you stay with me?"

Aisha knelt down and wrapped her arms around her man. She felt a ring being placed on her hand. As she drew back, she could see the evidence of his proposal. Gracing her ring finger was the largest, most beautiful mix of diamond and sapphires she had ever seen. Proof of her Fou Fou's love.

"Yes, Fou Fou. I will stay with you."

Fouad was overjoyed. After his long years of bachelorhood, his Aisha had just said yes. But his divided mind also knew his life had just become more complicated. Earlier, he fired his team. On account of Rachel. Now, he was planning a second operation. Would he be able to protect Aisha as he continued to seek Palestine's freedom? He lacked the stomach for gratuitous violence; he would not brook mistakes that resulted in the murder of innocents. But what of his own family? Could he keep Aisha separate from his dangerous agenda? Fouad forced his mind back to the happiness of the moment. Tonight, it was Aisha's night. For too long, she had been his woman without the respect matrimony affords.

Knowing Fouad al Najimi in New York City years earlier sparked Anne's desire to leave her comfortable Connecticut home with her insurance executive father and country club mother, to travel the world and reinvent herself. As with other westerners before her, once she arrived, the sands of the Middle East spoke to her. The history, the mysteries, the unfamiliarity – all beckoned. In the Middle East, she rarely was bored. She felt herself always wanting more. More knowledge. More belonging. More everything. Including her Fou Fou.

Slowly, she transformed herself from Anne to Aisha, known across the Middle East for her dancing skills. Her costumes, enviable figure, and hypnotic movements, soon placed her in steady demand in Cairo's international nightclubs well attended by tourists and Saudi high rollers out for a good time.

One of her favorite venues was a club high in the Muquattam Hills overlooking the pyramids and the Sphinx. "Son et Lumiere," a technical display of sound and light, flickered nightly across the desert, silhouetting the famous structures. Added to the show were the fine cuisine and dancing to French love songs on a terrace overlooking the pyramids. Inside, Aisha entertained to the haunting Egyptian tunes of Umm Kulthum.

It was there that she danced for her Palestinian attorney, on leave from his New York law firm. Soon, the pair became a couple, a perfect match of complementary idiosyncrasies and insecurities. Both possessed multiple national identities and allegiances. Both were exploring the world, wanting to play meaningful roles without quite understanding what they might be. Both forged their own unique set of ethics and beliefs. Fouad and Aisha, once one moved past their strikingly handsome appearances, were extremely serious individuals.

Cairo became the meeting ground on which the two forged their romance. The adoption of the city became a way for each to find at last a home for themselves. Each was the other's safe haven. The very qualities and conditions that set each one apart from others in the world were the very things that brought them familiarity and comfort in each other's arms.

No differently than the average American suburban husband whose inattentiveness hasn't gone unnoticed, Fouad had some ground to make up with

Aisha. The matter of Rachel's death made him think long and hard about his slowness to marry. He knew his unexplained silences and moodiness had not gone unnoticed. At last, he planned the romantic trip to the island of Cyprus. For Aisha. His wonderful American lover. Who would finally become his wife.

But more than a wedding would take place on Cyprus during this trip. Fouad's debt to his grandfather also was on his mind. He needed to meet with someone. While the marital festivities would be innocent, merry and long overdue, his meeting would be far more serious.

But equally overdue.

Sometime after his arrival on the island and his wedding in a Catholic chapel there, Fouad would continue his work for Palestine. Romance would be the perfect cover for a certain business transaction he needed to make. The orange trees of Cyprus would serve to remind Fou Fou of his grandfather. The scent his Aisha would wear would be his favorite -- orange essence mixed with jasmine. Grandfather and Aisha. Together in time and place.

30

"May I?"

Aisha's flowery perfume preceded her before she spoke. The belly dancer from the hotel was standing at Rossie's table at Groppi's. Over the weeks, the two Americans had shared glances. There was no mistaking their affinity. Both were homesick. Both sensed the other might be a friend. If only . . .

It was Aisha who broke the ice. She picked up Rossie's red leather- bound book of Bedouin poetry.

"My fiancé reads to me from this very book. I had to say hello. We have so much in common. I am Anne. From Connecticut."

The beauty held out her perfectly tanned slender arm, gold bangles slamming together, for an American handshake. Her manner was most un-Middle Eastern. A stunning diamond and sapphire engagement ring caught the light.

"Ken Rossberg. 'Rossie,' actually. Yes, from New York. Please won't you join me?"

The woman immediately retrieved her coffee and plopped herself down, again with all the grace of a college coed. Coltish, frisky, open. Gone for now were the sensuous affectations of the belly dancer. Rossie in a rush remembered how he missed his own culture.

"You speak Arabic."

It was not a question, but a statement. Rossie answered her in Arabic, confirming her suspicions.

"Yes. I have been a student of the language and the culture for many years. As have you, obviously."

The girl threw her head back, laughing for no apparent reason, as acres of her blue-black hair cascaded over the back of her seat. They continued in English, the two Americans. Their conversation was polite and discreet. Rossie and Aisha discussed poetry this day. But Rossie knew who she was. She was Fouad's girl. "Aisha," belly dancer. "Anne," from Connecticut.

As she leaned forward to stir her coffee, a familiar necklace briefly fell away from her neck. In an instant, Rossie's suspicions came into sharp relief. It was identical to Rachel's necklace. At the same time, he recalled in a rush the orange he was given before being shoved back onto the busy Cairo street that day.

Ladies and Gentlemen of the Jury, consider the evidence: Aisha's dancing eyes reminded him of Rachel's high spirits. Fouad was Melvin's target. Surely now, he also was Rossie's. The one responsible for Rachel's death. Rossie needed no further clues. No fingerprint on a revolver. No DNA. The trouble with the truth is, when one meets it head-on, there is no retreat. Rossie knew. He was becoming friends with someone close to Fouad al Najimi. The circle of coincidence and danger was tightening.

With their warm meeting, another thing was clear: if Rossie and Aisha indeed were now linked by a terrorist named Fouad, and his dark agenda, she had no idea of it.

She was as she appeared. An innocent. A person not unlike himself, deep into the esoteric mysteries of the desert.

She seemed like a perfect friend for Rossie. Someone, at last he could trust. Someone he could understand. Perhaps one step closer to accomplishing his mission of revenge. This had gone on too long. Rossie was tiring of his own bile. He was no longer good company even for himself.

31

Cyprus

"Do you, Anne Isabella Kellogg take as your husband Fouad Nazeer al Najimi as your lawful wedded husband, to love and cherish 'till death do you part?"

Aisha was a vision in a Spanish lace mantilla worn over her long dark hair. The mantilla cascaded over her simple blush pink dress, lightly touching her tanned shoulders. Her beautiful eyes said it all – she was content, could relax now. Her Fouad had taken the leap. He would never leave her side. If she had ever doubted that, she now was reassured. Her beautiful blue-eyed Arab from Palestine.

Only Aisha could care for him as she knew he deserved. While Aisha never met Fou Fou's grandfather, as the years passed, she imagined he shared the old man's character. Her man seemed to grow deeper, more serious, but oddly sadder, as the years passed. Along with her vows, Aisha silently assumed responsibility. She promised herself and God to be a good wife to her Fou Fou. No Catholic priest could affect her resolve. No words could be more powerful than Aisha's own affirmation of devotion on this day.

The priest married the couple in a traditional Catholic ceremony in a small chapel near the ocean. Afterwards, Fouad, Aisha, and a wedding party of 20 friends and family, sipped champagne on their hotel's veranda. The porch was decorated with potted orange trees, fragrant floral arrangements, and magical twinkle lights that, as night fell, intermingled with the starry night.

"Fouad . . ."

"Please, call me Fou Fou. It's a family name. We are family now."

Aisha's father wanted a serious conversation with his daughter's new husband.

"We are very happy for you both, of course. At first, I know you understand, Connie and I had our doubts about this union.   . . . with the age difference, and all. But now, after getting to know you in New York . . . now . . . well, you have our blessing. We were just hoping we might convince you both to come home. Back to New York, that is."

"Sir, of course, you know my original home is in disrepair these days . . ."

"Yes, Anne has told us of your grandfather and your family's loss. We are heartbroken for you and everyone who was moved aside. The question, son . . . may I call you that now?"

The man paused for an answer. Fouad nodded. "Yes, of course."

"Fouad, you have family now. Not just our Anne. There are Anne's brothers and many others in America. There is a nephew. And Anne's great aunt in New York. We are yours now. But you are both so far away. A wedding in Cyprus is romantic. We get that. But now there is a lifetime ahead of the two of you. We hope there will be children eventually. I know you have no other family. I want to ask that you consider moving back to the states. With Aisha. With your new family."

Then, the insurance executive attempted to draw closer to his new son-in-law: "In-sha-allah."

Fou Fou appreciated the man's words. And his momentary attempt at Arabic. Of course, he had taken his only daughter from him. Removed her to a distant place. All Aisha's father was seeking was normality. While Fou Fou did not say so, he shared the man's desire. Normality. Family. Closeness. Belonging.

Later, a well-known Greek belly dancer performed, and more champagne flowed. She entertained the couple and their guests -- Aisha's Connecticut parents and brothers, several Palestinians, and Fouad's Egyptian friends, Ali and Abdu. No one in the happy wedding party had anything to do with terrorism, threats against humanity, or any other bizarre political actions. Certainly not the groom. Not this star-filled night.

Fouad's agenda could wait. Tonight was for Aisha and only for Aisha, his love. For fresh flowers strewn across their marital bed. For him to dedicate himself to her physical pleasure. To take his time. To concentrate on her. Because she was his life partner. In all things but one: his agenda. The only clues Aisha had as to that matter were his increasingly dark moods . . . his inexplicable silences. Those, she did not understand. But she intended to get to the bottom of things. Not from curiosity, but care. She would hold his hand and ensure his peace and happiness. That was her job now. One she took seriously.

As the festivities unfolded, an uninvited guest waited his turn with Fouad al Najimi. Melvin lurked inside the hotel, watching the bridal revelers. He did not care at all about some Palestinian's wedding. He was here solely for himself – on his mind was a life in Paris, made possible with Saudi money.

And two rowboats that were about to meet on a remote lake near the ocean miles from any world capitol. Nothing to see here. Move along folks.

32

United States Naval Research Lab, Washington, D.C.

Dr. Alberto Siriano, staff research physicist, worked on sophisticated mathematical equations often resulting in U.S. defense weapons. He performed his calculations from inside the tall secure walls of the United States Naval Research Laboratory, one of the nation's preeminent research labs located in Washington, on the shores of the Potomac River.

Those who would lobby the nation's law makers often flew over the lab as their planes landed at Reagan National Airport across the river. Occasionally, the planes' bolts worked their way loose, dropping unannounced into the otherwise secure NRL compound below. No scientists had yet been hit by the falling debris.

Dr. Siriano's latest discovery carried the potential for non-defense application. Accordingly, national and international science journalists were invited to the lab to interview him. A line of PhD science journalists came and went, ending with the New York Times' man. Finally, the lab's own in-house newspaper reporter entered.

"Dr. Siriano, thank you for making time for me today. I understand you have made quite an important discovery. I know that lab readers will be interested in learning the details."

The physicist began his description. It involved logarithms, equations, and other technical data commonly understood by average science reporters. The reporter interrupted him, mid-presentation.

"Dr. Siriano, actually I flunked high school chemistry, and I never took a physics course." The woman held her breath, wondering what the man's reaction to her confession would be. She added: "I'm afraid I'm unable to understand your description. I'm sorry."

At this news, Dr. Siriano didn't miss a beat. Proving a lack of arrogance, he stepped to his chalk board.

"No problem. I'll explain physics to you and then you will understand my discovery."

Whereupon the scientist made good on his promise. He calmly stepped to a chalk board. He explained. He drew pictures. Then he outlined his discovery in layman's terms. Once he had completed his description, the reporter, note pad in hand, rose to leave. But the scientist was not finished.

"Perhaps you have asked yourself how a man such as me might involve himself in developing dangerous defense systems. How can he reconcile such a thing?"

The reporter thought, 'not really, never gave it much thought,' but kept her thought to herself.

The man continued his mea culpa. "In high school, I knew science would be my field. But what sort? I couldn't stomach dissecting animals, so that let out biology. Of course, chemistry labs always smell bad. That left physics. Which, of course, consists of mathematical equations."

He paused.

"How was I to know that my work playing around with numbers might someday be used to create weapons of mass destruction?"

At this remark, the man stared out the window, lost in thought, no longer aware of the reporter as she rose to leave.

Later, of course, Dr. Siriano's work continued. Eventually, one of his discoveries was so great that no reporters would be invited to call on him. His work progressed solely under lock and key. Only his own retina admitted him to his office. As far as the world at large was concerned, Dr. Siriano had fallen off the planet.

In the government somewhere, his discovery was tested, re-tested, and stored in a vault for its unfortunate use should the need arise. Case closed.

However, there was a loose end that still required resolution - the inventor himself, Alberto Siriano. In due time, the arrangements were made. It was discreet and occurred on a street in Rehoboth Beach, Delaware, with the Atlantic Ocean's waves pounding noisily in the background. Dr. Siriano was delivered a lethal poison aimed directly at his heart with what looked like a long hat pin. The hospital later called it a heart attack.

But his brother knew better. A man schooled in "Company" business.

A man known to some as 'Melvin Hibbard.'

33

Rossie and Fouad were not the only men in Cairo bent on revenge. Melvin, it turned out, also had an agenda. The money he would get from selling his brother's invention, to be sure, would come in handy. But best of all, he would repay the mother fuckers responsible for his brother's untimely death.

In keeping with the nation's traditional compartmentalization of various security interests, the Siriano brothers were vetted and kept apart from each other. They worked for different agencies, on different continents. The defense establishment kept keen eyes on Alberto, while Langley monitored Melvin. Despite their best efforts however, the brothers remained close. Distance and busy lives did not matter. There were always their Parisian dinners.

Fraternal twins, it is known, are capable of reading each other from great distances. Melvin and Alberto were no different. If one had a severe headache, the other a world away, felt it. When Alberto died, Melvin was not immediately informed. But he boarded a New York-bound plane anyway. He knew something was wrong. He needed to be near Alberto.

As the years progressed, Melvin's clandestine government service fostered cynicism. As the saying goes, "In Washington, if you want a friend, get yourself a dog." Through the years, the brothers often overrode their handlers sharing their work secrets. Each knew how to beat lie detectors. Their primary allegiances were to each other, for life.

The twin Siriano boys shared everything, including sensitive materials. They worked together as one man in the employ of their government. Their communications didn't stop short of the country's black ops, such as Alberto's latest product. Unbeknownst to their 'handlers,' Alberto already had passed his latest discovery to his brother when they met in Paris before his death.

When Melvin returned to Egypt, he carried his brother's discovery with him. One more secret Hibbard kept close to his vest. A secret that might be negotiable at some point in the future. In Melvin's world, everything has its price. His attitude was 'What's mine is mine; what's yours is negotiable."

The lizard was content in his silent world of secrets, bank accounts, and revenge for a brother's assassination.

Alberto's latest development was re-posited within the layered discretion of the nation's security system, guarded by those who guard such things. But Melvin's copy was secreted in a secure safe deposit box in Switzerland. It waited for Melvin's wife's visit sometime in the near future. A mousy woman no one would watch, Judith. Her in her simple cloth coat carrying a small, sensible handbag.

Fouad's grandfather, it turned out, wasn't the only one who 'trusted in God but tied his camels.' Insurance policies are always a good idea. In all cultures and all times.

Despite Melvin's feelings about women as an inferior species, he catered to his wife. Judith hated the dry heat of the desert, and even more, hated third world capitals. In preparation for their retirement, Melvin already had situated the little woman in Paris.

To avoid suspicion, her accommodations on the rue des Entrepreneurs in the fifteenth arrondissement were modest. Melvin couldn't hold back a chuckle at the address. Who was a better entrepreneur than he, he thought: From Middle America to a flat in Paris. Not bad for an aging spy dining on Spaghetti-O's and greasy falafel.

Following his retirement, he would join her, and they would find a better place. But not too much better. Melvin knew better than to attract undue attention to himself or their circumstances. Their money would be safe where it needed to be -- in Switzerland.

As he rented his rowboat on an inland lake, he thought of Alberto. Of their youth. Of their innocent neighborhood boys' club in Michigan, with its secrets – hiding places, and the like. Their secrets continued throughout their lives. Both were patriotic . . . to a point.

But vestiges of their Italian heritage kicked in with a life-long practice of 'omerta.' Family always came first. The others could get in line.

Melvin shared his code with Fouad and Rossie. For each man, family trumped everyone and everything. While countries represent opposing interests -- political parties, ruling elites, underdogs, winners and losers, a unifying element all countries have in common is family. Family security. Family wealth. Family bonds. On this, in the unlikely event they ever found themselves sharing a cocktail together, the three men would agree.

As Melvin knew firsthand, countries defending their interests – turf, commerce, resources -- turn first to spy craft. Knowing the enemy, particularly by covert means, can divert expensive and harmful armed conflict. 'Plan B,' is war. The generals sold Plan B not as 'war,' but as 'limited military conflict.' In both strategies, though, men die. Lives are altered.

In the twins' post-modern world, technology created its own new set of problems. Alberto was privy to the blackest of defense weapons, having developed some of them. The idea men are a class apart, necessitating increased attention to the protection of state secrets. Scientists must be watched closely lest they go off the reservation, breach state secrecy, or talk too much. Such indiscreet individuals fall into a category not often discussed openly, known as 'Plan C.' For the uninitiated, 'Plan C' amounts to "dead men can't talk."

Still, Melvin had no proof. But he knew 'Plan C' was the cause of his brother's untimely death. Not cholesterol. Not an errant blood pressure reading as reported by an apologetic physician, shaking his head. More likely to Melvin, Alberto's untimely death was a delayed reaction to an excellent poison cleverly delivered by those who would protect and defend. Clearing up loose ends.

Repeating. Melvin had no proof.

Ma'aleesh. Melvin had his brother's legacy. Securely sitting in Switzerland awaiting its withdrawal for the right price.

34

Today would be the men's first face to face
meeting. Fouad was aware of Melvin's past surveillance.
He'd even come to recognize some of the Americans
Melvin sent to track his movements. He directed his men
to capture the professor as a message to Melvin: 'You may
be close. We're closer.'

Melvin and Fouad. Cat and Mouse. Awareness
level, high. Egypt is a small country, telescoped in Cairo
with its elite international community. Friends tell friends
what they need to know. The watched are the watchers.
People know people. There are few secrets.

As Fouad rented the boat for his assignation, the
newlywed was having second thoughts. The day before,
he married an American girl, 'Anne Kellogg,' his 'Aisha.'
Her parents, 'the Kelloggs,' were vintage Connecticut,
with their crisp Brooks Brothers attire and obvious ease.

And there was Rachel to consider. Another American.
His friend is now resting somewhere at the bottom of the
Mediterranean.

Finally, there was Rachel's husband to consider.
Fouad still owed the poor man an explanation, however
lame. He seemed to be surrounded by Americans lately.
As he came to terms with how and when to face Rossberg,
today on this remote lake, he redirected his attentions to
the matter at hand. As a well-respected attorney in a New
York law firm, he was contemplating committing a crime
of monumental and international proportions. Proceeding
with this transaction would put him in position to help his
homeland. To avenge his grandfather's loss.

But he would also harm America -- a country that
welcomed him, sheltered him, and schooled him. A
country that provided him with a career in the law. A
country that brought him two American lovers. Today he
was about to betray that country. He thought with disgust
he was no better than Melvin, a man intent on a fat
Parisian retirement. While Melvin's motivation was
financial, Fouad's was about family. Restitution.
Payback.

Fouad reviewed his logic one last time. Why America? Why do this to his adopted second country? No sooner had he asked the question, than he knew the answer. America led the others, each with their own historical, geopolitical hands in the mess. Israelis, Turks, Brits, French, Spanish, Italians, Germans. And Arab nations with their own reasons – Syrians, Iraqis, Jordanians, Yemenis, Saudis, Lebanese.

Add Russians and Chinese with their mealy mitts to the growing list. Not the Kurds, hiding in the mountains. Nearly everyone had an interest or stake in his grandfather's land. It was like a club. Fouad was well aware of the culprits' identities. He was simply targeting the latest player on the chessboard.

These were Fouad al Najimi's thoughts as he rowed out onto the Cypriot lake. As he approached the other kayak in the middle of the lake, a pelican dove for a fish in front of him. One way to view the bird's innocent act was that the pelican was trafficking in death. But wasn't the fish sacrificed so the pelican might live? What of Fouad's mission? At what point does revenge become a force of nature? He could see Melvin's small dark eyes as he approached.

K a r e n   H a g e s t a d   C a c y

35

Melvin spoke first. "Sayyid al Najimi."

Fouad responded: "Sayid Hibbard. Or is it 'Sayid Siriano?'"

At the mention of his real name, Melvin dropped his reserve, and an oar. No one outside of Langley knew his birth name.

"The C.I.A. is not the only organization with information Monsieur."

Touche. Point. Counterpoint. Thrust. Parry. The pleasantries apparently were over before they began.

Melvin recovered his oar and some of his composure. The lizard returned to his rock, hard-to-get, waiting for Fouad to come to him. His tone of mildly bored aggravation returned to him.

"Why exactly am I here, Najimi? I was of the understanding it was to discuss mutual interests. I cannot for the life of me imagine why some Palestinian with an ax to grind would ask me here to Cyprus. However," (sighing as he delivered his cover story,) "my superiors seemed to think it would be useful to hear you out. Please commence."

"Let's not play games, Siriano. You've overheard my conversations. You understand my situation. It is high-tech fear I am after. Not something to be utilized, only dangled in front of the West . . . something sufficient to get everyone back to the table. My grandfather's legacy demands nothing less."

Fouad studied the man in the other boat. Most Americans had open faces, and a certain unique strength humor affords. This man . . . this man was a piece of work. A man to watch.

Melvin moved the conversation along: "Nuclear?"

"No."

Melvin was surprised at the man's answer. What then? Why was he here?

Fouad explained. "I know there are many new state-of-the-art weapons systems that have been developed. I have heard that many of them you already have tested in Iraq and Afghanistan. My need is to frighten. Not kill. Tell me, do you have such an item for sale today?"

Noticing Melvin's obvious confusion, Fouad threw in the zinger: "I have considerable funds available. Dollars, Euros, gold -- whatever you need. It can be done."

Fouad dangled the money before the lizard's glittering eyes.

"From the Saudis, I expect."

At this, Fouad shook his head. Not for Melvin to know.

Melvin had no expectations, but he had to ask. Carefully now, measuring his words as though each were loaded with dynamite, Melvin closed in.

"You say you are merely seeking a scare tactic? Isn't it a little foolish to tip your hand to me in such a way? You know I shall carry this weakness back to my handlers. Why be stupid? Is this what we taught you at Princeton?"

Spies and counterspies never speak the truth. What was Fouad's angle? The possibility of being played was high.

Fouad continued. "I understand you and your wife enjoy Paris. A pied a terre there can run quite a few Euros these days. You know I am your potential banker. So, let us not discuss morality or cleverness here today. You want something that I have. And I want something you have. It is only a matter of negotiation. Let us drop all of this nonsense."

Silence filled the lake. On the shore some tourists were taking pictures. At least, they appeared to be tourists.

"Fine. What I have is currently locked away from the world. A formula for something to be used someday when necessary. Do you understand the sun, Najimi?"

Fouad stared at his negotiator.

Melvin continued. "Sunspots?"

Fouad was lost. What did that have to do with a sophisticated weapon system?

Melvin began to deliver his brother's simplified version. The world would believe an errant sun storm had knocked out a country's electrical grid. Computers, lights, power, transportation. The targeted country could be reduced to the Dark Ages in an instant. No one would be killed. But the target would never be the same again.

Fouad was impressed. No one gets killed. A one-off device to scare those clever diplomats. Enough perhaps to convince them to re-carve Palestine. Back to original borders. People could get their land back. Walls instead of tent flaps. No one gets killed. Grandfather would be pleased. He was having difficulty containing his excitement at Melvin's offer.

"What currency are we talking?"

Their talk from here became more specific, and more profitable for Melvin. Walls were breached. Promises made. The deal was set. Melvin would be able to retire to Paris with his nagging wife. At least in Paris, he would be able to break free and spend large amounts of time in sidewalk cafés, nursing cappuccinos and watching pretty girls.

On shore, the man carefully replaced his lens cap. The long-range camera was returned to the picnic basket. An hour later, he boarded his flight out. If one wishes to navigate around the Middle East, Cyprus is known as its neutral 'no man's land,' the passport checkpoint allowing safe passage. Some flew to Cairo or Beirut from Cyprus. Others flew to Tel Aviv.

Back at the resort, seated on the veranda waiting for her new husband, Aisha had an important secret to share. She ceased taking precautions the moment there was a ring on her finger. And now, she needed to tell Fou

Fou the news -- he would soon be a father. Knowing how he felt about family, that he had lost his own family, she was certain a child would bring him peace. A baby might alter the dangerous course her new husband had set for himself. She knew he'd released his small army of comrades, rough men she intensely disliked. Perhaps a new family would help her husband adopt a more positive and conventional life.

At the same time, she knew her new husband was no boater. There could be only one reason for him to leave her for an outing on a Cyprus lake. He was meeting someone. While she shared his anger at international politics, she was now less sure than ever that one man could change the world. Wasn't it already on a trajectory of death and disappointment? Shouldn't the Palestinians call it a day? Wasn't it all too little, too late?

On their second night of married life, Fou Fou and Aisha dined on the terrace of the hotel by candlelight. Aisha spent her afternoon setting up the evening. A bowl of oranges graced the table. Fou Fou's favorite meal was turning on a spit. The lemon and rosemary of roasting lamb scented the night air. Two bottles were on ice at the table – one was champagne. The other was sparkling water. As Fou Fou began to pour the champagne, Aisha held up her hand.

"Fou Fou. I know that this is a little soon to be telling you such a thing. But I have news."

"Yes, my love. What is it?"

Silently, Aisha reached across the table, took his hand and gently placed it on her stomach. There were no words for this. A day like no other. Dark and white. Death, followed by life. On this day of setting wheels in motion to alter the world's map in favor of Palestine, Fouad's grandfather was about to become a great grandfather.

'In sha allah.' 'God Willing.'

36

Rossie moved a couch away from the wall. A nest of spiders had taken up residence, and he intended to offer them alternate accommodations in the Nile River. One large spider was crawling along a translucent thread to a hiding place beneath the couch. Rossie up-ended the furniture to get at the insect with a wet sponge. Intertwined with the spider's nest, he discovered a second nest, this one made of wires. There was a small antenna in the mess. Where was the trust, he thought.

In short order, the spiders, electrical wires, antenna all flew over the houseboat's railing in a jumble. Rossie searched room by room, locating more wires, and they, too, took a swim in the filthy, bacteria infested waters of the Nile.

As he rested from his important work, Rossie nursed a Stella Beera, fresh from the cooler. There was a knock on his door. No one visited him. Except perhaps Werner looking for his rent money. Two men stood in front of him. One was Werner.

"This is not about the rent. Mind if we come in?" Werner rudely pushed his way inside.

The other man was tall, well over six feet. His naturally blonde hair was sun-bleached to an unnatural platinum shade. His blue eyes were sharp and intelligent. Another Israeli pretending to be Swiss? The man's greeting cleared the air.

"Name's Isaiah. Shalom." The man extended his hand.

Rossie answered in Arabic, "Marhaba," in an instinctive move to create separation between himself and the intruder. Rossie retained his Jewish- ness solely for himself. It was not something he used as a calling card. This man was unknown to him. At any rate, Rossie hated pretension of any sort, especially when it was based on ethnicity. His strict view in this regard probably accounted for his study of the Arab language and culture. Unlike for many, Rossie's faith served him not as a restriction, but as an opening. He could be a Jew and move freely at the same time. It was this openness that led him to study the ancient cultures of the Levant. Like Rachel, he had no self-imposed boundaries.

That was Rossie's story. Now, who the hell was this?! Werner was moving towards the door. With a wave of his hand, he was gone, leaving Rossie alone with Isaiah, who stepped inside, casually placing a canvas bag on the coffee table between them.

Rossie crossed the room and leaned against his desk. Carefully, he slid one of the drawers open, revealing his guns.

The man, a trained Mossad officer, watched him carefully, ready for anything. Not so fast, he thought.

Isaiah slowly turned his bag without lifting it from the table, so its top was facing Rossie. He flipped back the flap making the purse's contents visible to Rossie. He pulled out a large black and white photograph.

In English, "Know these guys?"

Rossie recognized the two men in rowboats. One was Fouad, the other was Melvin. What the hell?!

Rossie answered in Arabic, "And if I did?"

"We need your help, Mr. Rossberg."

Who's 'we'?"

"Ma'aleesh." (Later, never mind.)

Rossie continued in Arabic. "Look, Isaiah. I do not know you. I barely know Werner. Why he thought he could just traipse in here with you I cannot for the life of me, . ."

Isaiah answered now in Hebrew: -- what was this, a war of languages? "I represent your people."

"Americans? Somehow I doubt that." Rossie was playing with the man. It was mildly amusing. Momentarily, it gave him the upper hand.

Now in Arabic, "Sayid Rossberg, you know very well that is not the case. Think about it."

Rossie hated the man's assumptions. "I am an American. My religion is no one's business but my own."

The man took a seat on the sofa, uninvited. "May we continue in English now? I believe we have established our linguistic abilities."

"You are Mossad. I might a' known you guys would show up sooner or later."

"Then you must know what this is about."

"Fouad and Melvin in two boats on some lake? The Palestinian and the C.I.A. officer duck hunting together? You're the one with answers. You tell me."

Rossie took a chair. He could relax; Mossad probably wasn't there to do him harm. But they definitely did want something. Who did they think he was? Still an American spy? Those days were now over. He could help no one. His eyesight was worsening, which meant his aim might not be too good. His body was filled with alcohol, making him calmer, but infinitely less adept. Mossad was crazy if they thought . . .

"Yes, my friend. Of course. Let me begin with this: We are thorough, we know all about you. Your politics – mostly liberal, we think. Your religion – at best, a 'holiday Jew.' Your intelligence – high. Your personal life – lately a wreck. Your wife, the real reason you are in Cairo, to avenge her murder at the hands of Islamic terrorists. How am I doing so far?"

"Go on."

The man rose and helped himself to a beer from the cooler. Before opening it, he raised it to Rossie as a question.

"Go ahead. Make yourself at home."

"We have a proposal for you. If you will agree to assist us with our mission, we will see that you have direct access to Mr.al Najimi. We understand you have unfinished business with the man. Unlike your United States of America, Israel is less -- how may I say it delicately – squeamish, about certain matters . . . life, death and revenge . . . these we regard as personal issues."

At this, Rossie interrupted him. ". . two eyes for an eye . . ."

"Exactly. So, we will not be interfering with any business you might have with the man. Hell, we might even help you brush up on your aim. We have your target practice print out from the Delta . . . you could use a bit more training, my friend."

The two men took a break. Each enjoyed his beer. Each took the other's measure. Rossie was an Arabist. But an Arabist with a purpose – payback. If he could help the Jews, depending on their project, and learn to shoot straight in the bargain, why not? He no longer felt a particular allegiance to any country. Only to Rachel's memory. He waited for the man to continue.

Isaiah pulled out a Mossad identity card from his wallet and laid it on the table.

"We have arranged a briefing for you tomorrow. As you may imagine, these matters are delicate. You will drive northeast through the Delta to the town of Ismailia on the west bank of the Suez Canal – just south of Alexandria. On the beach you will meet our man, Moshe,

at noon. He will be wearing a red scarf. When he smiles,
a gold tooth will gleam in the Egyptian sun. From
Ismailia, Moshe will direct you . . . naturally, your travel
plans and ultimate destination must remain confidential.
Moshe will be waiting tomorrow, Ismailia, at noon. Don't
be late."

The man rose abruptly and was gone before Rossie
had a chance to answer.

Rossie grabbed the gin bottle and poured. Beer
suddenly seemed insufficient. He struggled to regain his
bearings. Exactly where did he belong? Which tribe
would claim him? He picked up "The Prophet," a book
he was rereading before Werner broke in.

An oddly prescient sentence jumped from the
page: "And he said: No man can reveal to you aught but
that which already lies half asleep in the dawning of your
knowledge."

Rossie's eyes closed over the words. Somewhere
deep inside, he knew he was on the right path. But what
might that path reveal? Perhaps Mossad would help him
sort it all out. He considered an old decision to fall away

from religion. To judge Israel as one would any other country. He had not sought out 'his people.' 'His people,' it turned out, were seeking him out.

Some say 'Shalom.' Others say 'Salaam.' America says 'Peace.' Who among them really means it?

Ma'aleesh.

224

37

Near Ismailia, Egypt.

The narrow, one lane road heading north out of Cairo through rural Egypt's delta was clogged with goats, chickens, donkey-pulled wagons, and children playing. Egypt's fertile agricultural delta, a triangle of land fed by fingers of the Nile River, is an area critical to the sustenance of northeastern Africa. Here in Egypt the mighty Nile River ends its 4,163- mile journey from its southernmost source, a spring in the African village of Burundi. The Nile River is the world's longest river, flowing oddly northward, feeding and sustaining some 250 million people along its way.

To many, the Nile delta is a symbol of man's relation to his fate: 'The Nile rises. The Nile falls. Mahleshe. No worries. We are not in control of such matters.' For historical sociologists, much of the maddening insouciance of the Arab street can be explained by this ancient form of fatalism, with man's efforts forever tied to the twin follies of God and nature.

On their way, occasionally, cars would pass Rossie's car traveling much too fast. With only a low berm separating the water from the rough road, cars often swerve and sink into the canal beside the crude road. Rossie had a good driver, a man he knew well, and so here they were, escaping chickens flying by the car's windows, as his man laid on the car horn. The trip was nerve wracking. Travel from Cairo northeast to Ismailia, a distance of 40 kilometers, on a decent road might have taken just a half hour. But these were 'hard' kilometers; they'd be lucky to make the trip in two or three hours.

Enroute, Rossie sent an e-mail to his son:

"Son – On my way out of town for a short break and some sightseeing. Should be gone for about a week. I'll call you from there. No worries. Shalom, Dad."

Ken Rossberg, Jr. would know his father's destination. 'Shalom,' a word rarely used by Rossie in ordinary conversation, was their secret password. It meant he was headed for Israel. The two established several code words before Rossie left home – words to be used under duress, or other odd circumstances. For an Arabist in the employ of the CIA in Egypt, travel to Israel via the Sinai desert, qualified as such an odd circumstance.   Others had to negotiate their way from Egypt to Israel via the Greek island of Cyprus.

The dusty town on the Suez Canal was no different than ever. Sleepy, hot, dirty. A mix of chickens, camels, donkeys and shiny black Saudi limos. A strange place by any measure. Rossie had never been to Ismailia. But he recalled Rachel spent a holiday here once and swam in the canal.

Moshe, as described, was easy to spot sitting in a rowboat, wearing a red scarf. As promised, a gold tooth shone in the sun as he smiled. He motioned them to follow him. He scrambled from the little boat, raced up the bank of the canal and headed for a shack, removing his scarf as he ran. Inside, he again smiled as he began putting on a Saudi peasant headdress. He thrust the same costume at Rossie.

"Put it on. Have you ever ridden a camel?"

"No. I gather today's the day?"

Moshe nodded. His man held the two creatures by their tethers. He urged Rossie's ride to kneel down. Rossie carefully mounted his camel. His gun rubbed into his thigh. Ever the observant Mossad officer, Moshe held out his hand.

"You won't be needing that. We have made all necessary security arrangements. Have your driver return it to Cairo."

Rossie handed the revolver to Moshe.

"And the ammo, my brother."

He handed over a paper bag filled with ammunition he had secreted inside his shirt.

With these tasks out of the way, they were off, in a cloud of camel dust. Two men -- one a trained killer, the other a grieving husband, together on an adventure. The dunes of Sinai awaited them. A mile overhead, an Israeli satellite kept watch as they set out on their hot journey.

The lop-sided movement of his camel grew tiresome after only the first mile. Moshe kept up a steady pace; when Rossie's camel slowed, Moshe took the camel's reins to speed things up. After four hours of hot sun and no change in scenery, they stopped at a desert oasis, marked by one lone palm tree and a mountain of discarded tin cans.

Here, Moshe erected a small tent. They waited.

He heated and served steaming cups of Egyptian sweet tea. As they sipped the tea, a helicopter suddenly appeared, hovered over them, and quickly landed. Moshe ushered Rossie onboard. Rossie noticed with relief the aircraft's excellent air conditioning system.

At the same time, inexplicably, Egypt's radar shut down. International flights carrying important businessmen into Cairo Airport were kept circling overhead. An executive jet was told to stand by for further instructions. Tower technicians called for radar back-up.

But no worry. In no time, the airport's watchful beams were restored. They displayed the usual innocent business aircraft located exactly where they were supposed to be. The businessmen were able to make their cocktail hour at Shepheard's Hotel. No worries. All was restored to order. The nation's security system, such as it was, was returned without fanfare.

Rossie watched as the Mediterranean passed below the helicopter. After about a half hour, desert turned into roads, then houses, and finally into the metropolis of Tel Aviv, as they landed back in civilization. Moshe and his charge were greeted on the tarmac by a driver in an ugly, nondescript Mercedes Benz, with chipped and fading mustard yellow paint, desert dust caked everywhere including the windows, inside and out. Its back seat was piled high with old newspapers and spent coffee cups. A tacky hula dancer doll swung from the car's rear- view mirror.

For one of the wealthiest intelligence services in the world, Mossad's method of conveyance appeared crude at best. Of course, it was designed to be that way, as the professor was thrust back into the clandestine world of international sleuthing. Rossie was once again out of his element, scheduled for a briefing like no other.

38

Nadi Gezira, Cairo

Melvin Hibbard leaned back in his wicker chaise lounge, iced Crème de Menthe in hand. He sipped the dark green elixir through a tiny cocktail straw. He was a rather odd sight, this big man in loud Hawaiian swim trunks with his girly drink. But today, Melvin couldn't care less about the effect he was having on others, if he ever had. On this day, the soft ruffling sounds of bank notes manually being transferred from a wire note to his safe deposit box in an estimable and discrete Swiss bank, did his talking for him.

Since 1882, men and women of means and leisure have lounged by the Gezira Club's adult pool, as polite servers dispensed spirits and reinforced members' views of themselves as wonderful, special people. The club, located on an island in the middle of the Nile River, very close to downtown Cairo's Tahrir Square, is a holdover from the days of the British Empire.

"Mad dogs and Englishmen, out in the midday sun."

The "Island Club" is a 150-acre refuge complete with polo fields, tennis courts, children's and adults-only swimming pools, and croquet-game manicured lawns. One enters the Gezira Sporting Club through the Lido, the club's main entrance. There, those who need not apply also need not enter. It was a life Melvin had grown accustomed to. A life he would now not have to abandon upon his retirement from government service.

Another trip to Cyprus would complete the transaction. Some of the funds were temporarily withheld, as was part of the weapons system information. Partners in crime need not trust one another. No one in this transaction was stupid. Each man played the chess game of life methodically and carefully. No one would get hurt. Certainly not America, since Fouad was only purchasing fear. Fear can pass in time. No harm. No foul.

At the end of the day, each man would get what he wanted.

The man who would sip his coffee on a Parisian city street would be unencumbered by guilt. As his brother's ashes were long since dispersed, Melvin would spend his years content in the revenge he had extracted from the faceless men who killed Alberto according to a rule book nobody ever saw, but which governed security systems the world over. Limit risk. Eliminate liability. Closet secrets on a need-to-know basis. The pyramid scheme of esoteric knowledge most always favors those in control at the top. Occasionally, men like Melvin slip through the system. How long they are allowed to remain is another story. One for later.

And what about the other man? The man who would stage an international incident, with threats and counter threats, the United Nations, and scurrying security men, would see in the mirror an honest man. A man who vouchsafed his grandfather's legacy. A man who set his people free. A man of estimable background, to whom much had been given. A man who would now expunge the feel of the sand in his teeth from his childhood. A man who would again don the suit of an attorney, and represent various clients, some richer than others. A man who, at the end, would walk away to a mundane life of wife, children, and yes, even the Gezira Club. A man who might even be able someday to visit his homeland unburdened of identity cards or armed security. To the newly free Republic of Palestine.

That was the plan.

39

"Shalom, Mr. Rossberg."

"Hello." Rossie couldn't get the chip off his shoulder. He very nearly responded in Arabic.

"I see your address of record is Bayside, Queens, New York. You must be tired from your long flight, sir." The clerk dealt gently with Rossie. He was used to tired and cranky travelers. As he efficiently clicked his computer, he rattled off the hotel's amenities.

Finishing his spiel: "Moshe here will show you to your room."

Rossie whirled around to see his escort from earlier now dressed as a servile Hilton Hotel porter.

"Sir?" Moshe took Rossie's bag as the deskman handed him Rossie's room key.

Rossie addressed the clerk, "Moshe? Moshe's your bellman?"

With a hint of a twinkle in his eye, the hotel man responded. "Yes, Mr. Rossberg. This is *our Moshe.*"

Rossie caught the distinct emphasis on *'our.'* So, this was a Mossad hotel. Why didn't they just say so? Rossie played along as Moshe showed him to his room. After his bag was placed in its rack, the temperature adjusted, and the drapes opened, Rossie addressed his guide.

"You realize of course how silly this 'cops and robbers' scene is?"

"Tomorrow. Get some sleep. I'll see you out front at 9 a.m. You are our guest. Order room service. The food's pretty good here. Shalom, Sayid Rossberg. And welcome to Israel."

The next day, Moshe met him in the ugly yellow car and drove him through the busy streets of downtown Tel Aviv to his meeting. The lobby of the multi-story building they entered was large. The Bank of Israel and several other companies were housed on the main level. At the far end of the lobby, past a noisy cafeteria, there was an unmarked door. This is where Mossad officers clocked in for work. Moshe ignored the door, leading Rossie to a dentist's office on the third floor instead. From there, they took a janitor's door to a back stairwell.

Mossad's headquarters were actually a building inside a building. The company had its own power supply and its own water and communications. They shared nothing with the Bank of Israel and the other tenants except the lobby and newsstand with the blind clerk. At least he appeared to be blind.

Moshe led Rossie up two more flights of stairs, and then to an elevator to the tenth floor. Unseen from the hallway were Mossad's team of analysts, psychologists and planners. Emerging from a long, windowless hallway, the men were greeted by a secretary and directed into a briefing room. There were comfortable leather swivel chairs, world maps, and a bank of video screens along one wall. There was a slight whir of a motor in the quiet room, indicating something was operational. Rossie glanced up as a ceiling mounted camera lens automatically focused on his face.

After several minutes four men entered the room and took seats.

"Shalom, Mr. Rossberg."

"Yes, hello."

"Moshe, you may be excused now. Good job. Thanks very much."

At this, his traveling companion was escorted from the room.

"I'm Josh. Your case has been assigned to me."

Case? What case? Since when was I a case? thought Rossie.

Josh had before him a thick dossier. As he began speaking a large wall-sized screen lit up showing slow motion photographs of Rossie's life – Rossie receiving a diploma, Rossie's wedding, Rossie and Rachel walking young Ken in a pram in Central Park, Rossie at a symposium of Middle East experts. These guys knew Rossie's life better than he did!

"Of course, all of Israel shares in your recent grief."

Josh waited. The silence in the room was deafening. Rossie was not about to break it. What were they up to anyway?

"We have been aware of Fouad al Najimi for many years now. A remarkable man who somewhere has gone off the rails."

More silence.

"Let's be real here, Rossberg. We know very well why you are in Cairo. And it's not for the fine cuisine or the soft desert nights. Is it?"

Rossie said nothing.

"Know anything about this?" Josh pointed up at the wall.

One picture replaced the images of Rossie. It was the same photograph Isaiah showed him in Cairo -- Fouad and Melvin. He knew who they were. Why pretend he didn't?

"No."

"They are up to no good. We believe Siriano may have in his possession . . ."

Rossie interrupted. "Siriano?"

"Melvin's last name. Melvin Siriano. Hibbard's his 'stage name.' Alberto Siriano, his fraternal twin brother, was a scientist. Alberto, we believe, developed a particularly noteworthy weapons system before he died."

Rossie's disinterest in the meeting was growing stronger by the minute. So, what? Why tell him? Who died and put him in charge of U.S. intelligence?

The silence in the room was broken by the steady tick tock of a large wall clock. Just five minutes had passed since the meeting had begun.

"We believe that's what al Najimi's up to. That meeting in Cyprus captured by our cameras was a transaction."

"Why tell me? Why not tell U.S. authorities?"

"Rossberg, we are not necessarily interested in stopping this sale."

Sale? What sale?

"Our interest lies in securing the technology for ourselves. In case of some dark day in the future."

Was there a summary of this he should have read before the meeting?

"You can understand that there would be no point in anyone being aware of our possession of this weapon. And that is where you come in."

Rossie made no attempt to disguise his sarcasm:
"As a fellow Jew."

More silence. Rossie was listening so carefully
that he developed a spasm in his back. Again, with the
presumption of his beliefs, his allegiances. How about
faith to the truth, scholasticism? How about hearing the
other guy out? His liberalism kicked in. Sure, Israel had
their arguments. So, did the Arabs. His interest was not
in modern politics. His interest was in the somewhat
removed world of calligraphy. Of the mysticism of desert
poetry. Of the culture of the region. Why didn't anyone
get that?

Besides, this conversation was way above his pay
grade. He had no interest in,

Josh spoke. "You haven't asked about Melvin.
His role in this."

"Perhaps it was an innocent meeting. Our country
is allowed to meet with people in Cyprus, last time I
checked. Assuming the meeting wasn't on the up and up,
why involve me in this? I'm liable to go back and tell
Melvin, aren't I?"

"Look, there is more information that further complicates our actions, and it involves you personally."

"Me?"

"Well, you and al Najimi specifically."

"Don't know the man. Why don't you ask Melvin?"

"Your wife knew al Najimi. Did you know that?"

Rossie should have stayed back on his houseboat. The sunsets, the wine, the . . .

"We think his men were responsible."

"Responsible . . ." Rossie didn't want to hear any more of this.

"We think al Najimi's men killed your wife. Against his orders, for what it's worth."

Rossie's hands clenched beneath the table. He wanted air. To be anywhere but here, in the bowels of Israeli security.

"We have been observing you and your family for many years now."

"Obviously." Rossie spat the word out.

Josh turned to a man standing at the door. "Get Mr. Rossberg a finger of brandy."

Rachel. Get to the point. Rachel. Rossie wanted to leave.

"There's more to it. Look here, Rossberg. You and al Najimi . . . about the same age, wouldn't you say?"

Rossie was quickly losing patience. What difference did that make?!

Josh continued, now looking directly into his eyes. What was this?

"There's no easy way to say this. Kenneth Rossberg, Jr., your son, is actually his biological son. Najimi's, that is."

Rossie gulped for air. The brandy was placed in his hand. Robotically, he downed the liquor.

"Have no doubt. We are correct. We have tested the DNA. Rachel was pregnant when she returned from Cairo. Think back: you two were married within a month of her return stateside. You thought Kenneth was premature. He was not."

Josh continued.

"We have done the tests. Discretely, of course. This must be a shock. But it should explain to you now, why we failed to end the situation on the lake when we had the chance. Easily done by our experts. There was you and your family to consider. We needed to have this talk with you before taking any action where al Najimi's concerned. We felt we owed you the courtesy."

"Easily done by our experts."

Even in a sensitive discussion, Josh couldn't resist his moment of boastfulness about his organization's power to eradicate certain persons at will. Rossie had a distinctly unscholarly thought: Maybe he and Melvin should go fuck themselves. Where was the moral high ground? Where was the trust?

Continuing, Josh leaned forward so that his face was inches away from Rossie's. "Let us review now, honestly."

Josh grabbed the bottle of brandy and poured Rossie another drink. As he continued, he tapped out each point with his pen on the mahogany table. The sound echoed against the room's walls. Rossie's hand jerked suddenly in a spasm, knocking over his glass. A man came from behind him, wiped the table and refilled his glass.

Josh continued.

"A: Fouad's men killed your wife. You want to avenge her killing. Very understandable: Allow us to be the first to offer our assistance with regard to that."

"B: Fouad's now part of your family, like it or not."

"There is a 'C.'"

Rossie thought he had stopped breathing. What if he died here in this room? Would they notify Kenneth? Would they ship the body back Stateside, or would the Jewish custom of swift burial supersede his wishes? These were Rossie's disembodied thoughts . . .

Our 'C." We want that weapons system. We must have it. You can see, Rossberg, we have something in common here."

Rossie struggled to open his mouth to speak. "Who knows?"

"No worry. Fouad has no idea of his relation to your son. We have it on good authority he ordered the hit on the ship. But his orders specified no deaths. The man's Ivy League, an international attorney. Smart guy, but he lacks the stomach for the hard stuff."

Josh's neutral tone was distressing. Rossie hated Josh nearly as much as he hated Fouad. And Melvin. The list of his least favorite people was growing rapidly. Josh was still talking. Would the man never shut up?

"Of course, we have it on good authority . . ."

Good authority? What authority? Melvin?

" . We understand him to be extremely distressed about what his men did to Rachel. A huge mistake by his team. We do know, and we are sharing with you, that your wife's death was the last thing intended by al Najimi. Fact is, he had no idea she was even a passenger on the ship. He since has fired all of his men. We had hoped the shock of this event might lead him to rethink things. Until we saw this. The man was just married . . . oddly enough . . . to an American girl. I think you know her – Aisha. On the island of Cyprus. The same island where just last week we shot these pictures."

Josh pushed a large black and white photo across the table. The bride, Rossie's new friend. The circle closed. Aisha and Fouad. Married. Somewhere a voice spoke to Rossie. Technically, would that make the girl Kenneth's step-mother?

Josh could tell he was fast losing Rossie's attention. He leaned back in his chair, ending the meeting.

"Go now. Moshe will return you to your hotel. Please take some time to think. Process everything, we have discussed today. I must warn you, however, contact no one. Obviously, not Melvin. Certainly not your son. We need to continue our meeting back here tomorrow, at the same time. But first, out of respect, we want you to take time to consider things."

Rossie was struck by Josh's assumption of his silence. He was American, not Israeli. Why wouldn't he take this information back to his people? He knew the answer, and it made him angrier. Because he was a Jew, he would keep Josh's confidence. They were banking on his allegiance shifting to them. Welcome to Israel. How do you like the country so far?

The door of the conference room opened. Moshe entered and escorted Rossie from the room as he would a wounded animal. Not a distant analogy. Because Rossie was mortally harmed. His knees were wobbly. He thought he might throw up. His head was pounding from shock and the early application of alcohol. It was 10 a.m., and he hadn't eaten breakfast yet.

Josh followed them from the room.

"Let me leave you with something else, something we like to say here: 'There is no truth in Cairo; only versions.'"

'Rachel.' 'Kenneth.' 'Fouad al Najimi.' 'Josh.' 'Melvin.' 'Aisha.' Names and words thrashed around in his mind. Moshi escorted him to his hotel room. He drew the curtains as one would do for any sick person. No need for the harsh Mediterranean sun today. Softness, quiet, meditation was needed. What was required now was darkness. A safe room in which to contemplate dark thoughts. It made sense.

"I'll be downstairs in the lobby. If you want to talk. If you need anything, call room service. The tab's on us. Take care, my friend."

Moshe left Rossie alone at last.

40

"It is not with the claws or the beak but with
the wings that you go to heaven."
Charles de Ganay's family emblem and motto,
Fleury, France, 1961

Half an hour later, Josh had lunch at his corner
sandwich stand. He returned to the same conference room
where earlier in the day he met with Kenneth Rossberg.
Poor man. Josh switched on the recorder. He could hear
water running. He must be taking a shower. Good, Josh
needed a cup of coffee. He went down the hall to the
kitchen and fixed his coffee the way he liked it, with three
sugars and real cream. He returned to his listening post in
time for Rossie's expected call stateside to his son.

"Dad. I was waiting for you to call. You in
Israel?"

"As indicated. Yes, son."

Rossie sounded morose to his son. Flat.

"So, are you touring . . . or what?"

"This trip, son, has been about your mom. She was here in Tel Aviv several times in her life, you know."

"I remember. There was the time on a kibbutz when she dropped by to see me. I couldn't believe it!"

"Well, you always were her little boy, even after you entered your twenties."

"I know dad. I sure do miss her. And I miss you. I miss our family. When are you coming home? Haven't you learned enough by now?"

"As you have imagined, this is about nostalgia. Old places, old faces. Reliving your mother's and my time here over the years. You know many of our trips were taken separately, for our research. I've been retracing some of the steps she took without me."

"Are you about done?"

"Nearly, son. There're a couple more things I have to do before I return to New York. Please be patient with me."

"It's okay, dad. Whatever you need. I'll be here when you get back."

"Ken, you are our special, wonderful son. Nothing has changed. I love you dearly. We'll talk after I get back."

Kenneth sat alone in his mid-town office after the call. 'Nothing has changed.' That meant something most definitely had changed. Kenneth knew his father. Rossie wasn't the only Rossberg who could add.

Josh heard a click as Rossie ended the trans-Atlantic call.

A man of substance.

With the call, Josh gained further insight about his future asset. Rossie was a family man, first, last and always. He possessed impressive self-restraint. And, most importantly to Mossad, Rossie could keep a secret. This last finding was vitally important to Josh as he prepared to complete his recruitment.

41

"Kill one, frighten ten thousand."
Sun Tzu, Chinese strategist

Fouad and Aisha returned to their Garden City home, Aisha sporting her new wedding band -- a cluster of tiny diamonds complementing her spectacular engagement ring. Someone had moved her things in while they were away. As with all new brides, Aisha spent a considerable amount of time rearranging their home. Her feminine touches were welcomed by Fouad, to the extent he noticed them. Ornate mirrors went up to reflect the light in the evenings. Large vases of flowers appeared. Fouad was greeted home by soft jazz or Mozart music, the smell of home-cooked meals, and his Anne falling into his arms, laughing even before he spoke.

As he was before they left, Fou Fou was preoccupied. He wasn't sleeping through the night. He paced around as Aisha pretended to sleep.

Finally, she tried the direct approach: "Fou Fou, I need to ask you something."

"Anything, little mother."

Aisha's cobalt blue eyes met her husband's in a steady gaze. "Where were you?"

"When?"

"You know. In Cyprus. Boating, Fou Fou? Boating? You?

"I took a walk by the lake. There was no boat."

Fouad hated to begin his marriage with a lie, but he knew it was to shield Aisha from any danger. The less she knew, he felt, the safer she would be, from whomever.

"Really." Aisha's solemn statement conveyed her feelings. I don't believe you. I cannot accept your story. This is not over.

"Yes. Please, Aisha. Nothing special. This once. Believe your husband."

He could see Aisha wasn't buying it. But he had to protect her, even from his own actions. Now there were two. His child also now needed him. Fouad's two families, the past one he was avenging, and this new one -- both fought for his attention. The fact that the two were incompatible hadn't yet occurred to him. For now, Fouad needed to keep his own counsel.

Later that night, a full moon shone into the living room window, carrying him back in time as he slept on the couch. He heard laughter, smelled a dinner being prepared at his desert cabana. The year was 1964. Fouad was at his desert place with his two best friends, Ali and Abdu, and their American friend, Rachel. Their easy camaraderie spilled out over Cairo's desert dunes in gales of laughter. The three young men were well known for their silly antics around town.

Ali and Abdu were regaling Rachel with a story about Fou Fou's driving skills.

"Listen, Rachel, Fou Fou cannot drive in the Delta anymore." Ali set up the story as Abdu refilled their wine glasses.

Abdu continued. "I wish you could have seen him drive into that canal. You know, Fou Fou, your hair doesn't look so good when it's wet!"

Fou Fou attempted a defense. "I was trying to avoid a goat."

Laughing, the two friends played to Rachel's appreciation: "Fou Fou, you are the goat."

His trusted friends went back to 'the good old days.' So close were the three back then, if one were to commit a murder, the other two would be likely to ask what the man did to provoke him. None of them engaged in anything more than childish college pranks, most often pulled on each other. They were fairly moral men. Even early on, Abdu and Ali used their high-jinx to rouse Fou Fou from his moods. Their nights out watching local belly dancers were fueled by alcohol and raucous, but well-meaning humor delivered in Italian, French, Arabic, and, on occasion, the King's English.

As college and adulthood separated the three, only Fouad became 'radicalized.' His moods seemed to ebb and flow according to the latest atrocities that occurred in his former homeland. Middle East politics were not an abstraction for Fou Fou. They were vehicles that transported him instantly back to the dusty tents of his childhood. To his disenfranchised family.

Abdu and Ali were not involved in Fouad's early attempts at settlement – a couple of harmless hostage takings for media attention, with the hapless prisoners being returned to their families with sacks filled with oranges. The ship take-over was another matter. Rachel was one of them. She was a member of their merry band of carefree twenty-somethings running around Cairo, hitting the clubs, climbing pyramids with their car windows and doors thrown open to hear the French music playing down below.

Soon enough, talk on the streets confirmed to Ali and Abdu that the tragic mistake onboard the ship was performed by Fouad's men. In an intervention, the men turned on Fou Fou, accusing him. Fouad briefly roused himself from the couch. Sinking back, his mind filled in the missing years. After Rachel's death his friends all but disowned him. She was one of them. There was no piece of land in Palestine worth her loss. He recalled the men's last speech to him.

"Fou Fou, you walk with dishonor now. You cannot say 'my men, my men.' It was you who caused this. Allah knows we are friends forever. We will not leave you. Even though you deserve our silence. Here is our offer. You must stop it all. And speak to us. Complain. Swear. Rage. We understand your anger. But we will not accept your actions."

As the full moon lit up Fouad's ornate living room, he again recalled his friends' words. Their glasses were raised. The red wine commemorated her still vital body as it bled out from a hundred tiny fishes using it as their evening meal somewhere under the Mediterranean.

Ali spoke. "And to her son. We must remember she had a child, Fou Fou."

Abdu: "It is a serious thing. A burden we must never remove from our backs."

Then the three friends drank their wine, silently wishing time might be retrievable, that a single act of violence might be retracted.

"This, this will not do, Fou Fou. Now you've done it. You must stop now before someone else gets harmed." Ali was always the soft voice of reason in the group.

Abdu, the sillier one, also was shaken. "Fou Fou, Fou Fou, Fou Fou! Look what you have done! She was our friend, Fou Fou. Rachel! Our pretty, happy Rachel."

But they weren't finished.

Ali: "You must stop all this. We understand why. But now it really is too much, Fou Fou. Chalas'na. It's over now, finished. That's it."

Someone poured alcohol, and the three men continued past the moment. Past the moment perhaps, yet the moment never again would leave the friendship.

Through the early years, the men's friendship had been about joy, pranks, the latest Egyptian pop music. Riding around town, laughing. Rachel's murder changed all that. From that time forward, there was an undercurrent of tension, particularly as events unfolded in Palestine and Israel. The joy was still there for the men. But it was tempered now. They were older and wiser. And sadder.

42

"Abdu, it's time for another get-together. Just us three. Aisha will not be coming. Call Ali. I have ordered a fine meal. Friday. Don't be late."

It was a year since Rachel's death and Fouad was married. But in spite of everything, Fouad was still a prisoner of his past. He mistook his friends' steadiness for forgetfulness of the ship tragedy. He would soon be put right once again. Some things, even time cannot heal.

He ordered a sumptuous catered meal to be served in his desert retreat. Only the three friends attended. Under the stars, on a patio lit only by lanterns, the men enjoyed each other's company, the fine wine, the excellent cuisine. But his friends knew something was up. They knew Fou Fou. They could see it coming.

Fouad read their minds. "Please hear me out. But first, a toast to Rachel."

He needed to return them to his dark agenda once more. He needed their advice, and their commitment to friendship. He needed to confide in someone. He did not wish to burden Aisha. She was busy creating their child. And making a home for him. Fouad was a dead man walking, unless he did this one last thing. Unless he tried to get his land back.

Islamic terrorist? He was a law-abiding Catholic. A man who, but for circumstances, would be growing oranges and exporting them to Europe from his grandfather's farm. A man who now wanted children, a family of his own.

A man of peace.

Both Ali and Abdu came from old moneyed Egyptian families. Both watched as their families were stripped of their wealth by Gamal Abdul Nassar's nationalization of the country. Abdu recalled the day Nasser's soldiers came to his family's luxury apartment in the city and removed priceless works of art. The art pieces, Oriental rugs, and fine jewelry were never returned. All three men in varying degrees had experienced the pain of governments out of control.

Ma'aleesh, one must live, mustn't one? Swallow hard. Deal with it. "The Nile goes up, and the Nile goes down."

Ali, always the father figure in the group spoke.

"Have you thought about making restitution to the son? You know, Fou Fou, you really ought to do something more for Rachel's family. Such an act wouldn't hurt you either, my friend."

No answer. The three sat in silence, sipping their wine.

Ali, sensing something unusual, continued. "Fou Fou, what now? It's not over yet, is it?"

They knew Fouad too well.

"Not quite."

At this, the two men erupted in a litany of swear words beginning in Arabic, then moving to French, Italian and English. And back to Arabic. A few choice words were created, ones involving animals' reproductive organs. Words not used in any polite company anywhere on earth.

Finally coming up for air, Abdu shouted at him: "You honor Rachel in one breath, and then you begin with the devil in the next breath. Fou Fou, we are not with you on this. You know that. Nothing has changed."

"Please, hear me out. This is my one thing. It is well thought out. No one will get hurt. But the world's media will report. The diplomats will pay attention. Accommodations will be made. That's all. Chalas. Finished."

After Fouad spoke, there was a long silence.

"Merde! Really, Fou Fou, this is too much now. Ali, I'll be in the car."

Abdu left the patio, slamming its gate hard.

Ali rose to his feet.

"Fouad, you had better come to your senses, man. You are alone in this. Chalasna."

Ali stood over Fouad, then took his face in his hands. Slowly, with great friendship, he kissed Fou Fou once on each cheek, in the continental way.

"You are getting in too deep, my friend. Only God can save you now."

Then he too was gone.

Fouad was left behind with the rest of the wine and his own thoughts. It's better this way, he thought. They're right. I must do this alone. Friendship cannot cover such things. The lights of the stars and the burning lanterns burned into the night. They hovered over the desert and a sleeping Palestinian, many miles from Cairo. A man trapped in a life not entirely of his own making.

No one will get hurt.

43

If Rossie were a reluctant visitor to Israel, today, before his second session with the notorious Mossad, he was positively stubborn. Like a donkey tethered by a rope around his neck, his heels were dug in tightly to the earth beneath him. He brushed his teeth twice. Then, changed clothes. Then checked the international news. Then verified his bank balance. Anything to hold off the Israelis. He would be late. Too bad. They would just have to wait. At one point, he considered leaving altogether. Catch a quick flight to Cyprus.

He had about had his fill of these guys.

So much like Melvin.

Same faces, same games.

Different country.

Josh was waiting. This time there was fresh coffee, buttery rolls with strawberry jam. A pitcher of fresh orange juice sat at his place with a crystal goblet. 'These guys are pulling out all the stops,' thought Rossie as he took his seat.

Josh began reciting something in Hebrew: "But you do not see, nor do you hear, and it is well. The veil that clouds your eyes shall be lifted by the hands that wove it. And the clay that fills your ears shall be pierced by those fingers that kneaded it. And you shall see. And you shall hear."

Pleased with himself he sat back and waited for Rossie to speak.

"A quotation from Kahlil Gibran's 'The Prophet.' An Arab Christian poet. Translated into Hebrew. By a Mossad agent. Now who's confused? I know what you're doing. Playing to a scholar. It seems you know of my book on Gibran. You've researched me. I got it. Yesterday, true confessions. Today, Gibran. It won't work. I may support the State of Israel. I may have Jewish parents, and now it seems a half-Jewish son. But

I'm not one of your Israeli warriors. Please do not make that mistake."

Silence, as Josh and his deputy took in Rossie's words. His attitude. His absolute disinterest.

"Please, take a moment. Have some coffee. The rolls are fresh. As a New Yorker, there's one thing I think you'll concede. That our breads and pastries are the best in the world. There are no substitutes for Old World bakers. As much as classical music, fine art, education, and good bread also is a sign of high civilization."

Roping him in with congeniality. Perhaps it would work.

Josh continued. "Look, Mr. Rossberg. Yesterday was rough. For you to learn such things must have been very, very difficult . . ."

Interrupting, "My son is not my son. My wife lied to me. My son's father killed my son's mother. My son's father is a terrorist. My fellow Jews have torn what's left of my family away from me. Difficult, you say? Not even close, my friend. Not even close. And now you want my help? Me? A simple college professor? A widower? A child-less father?"

Josh let him run down. He poured him a glass of orange juice. He sat back, arms folded. No one could hurry this meeting beyond Rossie's ability to proceed. Fact was, Rossie was a free man. A man who now knew what they were up to. He could walk at any moment.

Today, the Israelis, so used to having the upper hand, sat, palms up, waiting patiently for the man's heritage to kick in. There was no guarantee it would. Professors were an odd lot. Allegiances were bred out of them. Accepted tomes were their watchwords. Not humanity's petty squabbles.

They were above all that.

Most of the time.

Psychological transferal, it's called. When a man takes his dire situation, his enemies, and transforms them at the first opportunity, no matter how much sense it makes. A man cuckolds you? A man steals your wife?

And your son? A man acts against your country, prepared to kill your friends and countrymen?

Mahleshe. Strike out and hurt anyone you can. The making of a revenge-nik. In some circles revenge-niks might be called terrorists. And so proceeded a slow psychological turning in Rossie's mind. Away from careful scholar. Away from dispassion. Away from the need to consider all sides.

Josh could see the change in Rossie's eyes as he sat up straighter, adding several inches to his small frame. Before his eyes, a damaged man became a partisan. A fighter. The university system was losing its grip on Kenneth L. Rossberg, Sr. Emotions were taking over. Revenge. Anger. Finally, there is a need for skilled partners with guns.

Josh stepped in. "What this all boils down to is we have a mutual interest in al Najimi and Siriano. Eventually, al Najimi'll pay a visit to you. Melvin? We'll keep an eye on him. All we want you to do is be aware of these two. They are in business, of that we are certain. We have an interest in the outcome. So, go home.

Continue on as before. But know that we will be nearby
until this matter's resolved."

"How will it be resolved?"

"Mr. Rossberg. We will give you the first chance
at this man. After that, go home to New York. Forget
about all of this. We will take it from there."

Rossie could see that Josh and Company were now
his newest allies. They could have continued without his
assistance. But they invited him here to tell him the rest
of the story. They trusted him. He felt a tug of emotion
as he realized his tribe was looking out for him and his
son. After a few more cups of coffee, the two sides forged
a tenuous partnership, a sort of mutual assistance pact.
They had told him what he needed to hear. He would
report back if there were any further developments in
Cairo.

Knowledge is a good thing. Most of the time.

44

"Who can separate his faith from his actions, or his belief from his occupations? Who can spread his hours before him, saying, 'This for God and this for myself; This for my soul and this other for my body?' All your hours are wings that beat through space from self to self."

"The Prophet," Kahlil Gibran

Rossie returned home to the houseboat. Everything was as before. The sunsets were still deep pink over the pyramids. The muezzins still called the faithful to prayer from Cairo's ancient minarets five times each day. Werner still carried his man-purse and was an irritating presence. He continued his silly charade around Rossie. The difference now though was that Rossie now knew Werner could and would shoot if circumstances required it. He was a highly trained Mossad agent. And they expected nothing less of their man.

Rossie was uncertain whether that fact comforted him or added to his dis-ease. It all depended on what happened, who was involved, and whether or not Rossie could complete his own mission: Rachel's final good-bye

The ground beneath Rossie's feet had shifted. He journeyed to Tel Aviv as Ken's father; he returned as Ken's step-father. Nature or nurture? He wondered. As he replenished his drink glass many times over the course of the next days, he revisited all the family years, taking a closer look at it all. At Rachel. Kenneth. Their lives together.

What he came up with in the end was that the first lie was the only lie. Their lives were real, close and spent together every bit as a family. Rachel was his loving wife. Kenneth was his devoted son. If some genetic interloper were to try to break those bonds, he would have another thing coming.

Still, while he came to Cairo to meet his wife's killer, the idea that he also would meet his son's father was nearly too much to take. Now not only must he settle up Rachel's loss at the Palestinian's hands. He also needed to greet his visitor with care on account of Kenneth. Now, shooting him had become more problematic. Still,

While he waited for the terrorist and newest member of his family to show up, Rossie spent his time plowing through a thick dossier Josh had given him before he left.

The name on the outside of the thick bundle, 'Fouad Al Najimi.'

The information only supplemented his decision about his dwindling family – he would not tell Kenneth of his Palestinian father. The son needn't know of his mother's indiscretion. He had no need of knowing Fouad's dark agenda. He could do without the knowledge that the man whose blood flowed through him killed his mother and left Rossie so damaged as to pack a gun and seek revenge in Cairo, many miles from his cosseted university life.

Rossie was certain: Kenneth needed no other father than himself. He would live a long and happy life as a Jew. No need to complicate matters. This family secret would be forever locked in Rossie's heart, and in the recesses of Israel's security center.

For now, . . . he waited. Based on their psychological profile, Mossad thought it likely Fouad would seek out Rossie in due course. And when that occurred, Rossie was to make a call to Funduq Hilton, to the two brash, noisy 'Americans' who were staying there. No one would mistake the pair for Mossad agents. Their devil blue-eyes showed who they were – arrogant Americans with more money than brains, here to tour the ruins. Anyone observing them might have as easily thought they were the ruins. Is this what western civilization had come to?

Each morning, they read their newspapers in the hotel's lobby before taking off on their archeological tours. They also took care of certain other matters and awaited Rossie's call. Their compadres, Werner and Isaiah, also waited beyond the foot lights.

If Rossie were to kill Fouad, a safe bet, all things considered -- the two Israeli 'cleaners would arrive at the houseboat. They would remove any trace evidence from the house-boat and spirit their fellow Jew safely out of the country and back to New York City.

Everyone would be happy. Rossberg would have his revenge at long last. And Mossad would have their hit with minimal effort.

Chal'asna. It's over.

The long desert sunset was at its final stages as Rossie settled back with some Mozart and a good book. To say a glass of wine sat beside him would be redundant. Someone was at his door, disturbing what little peace he had left. Who could it be? Werner snooping again?

It was Aisha. She thrust a box of fresh baklava pastries into his hands and stepped inside, loose, with her usual American-ness emanating off her in optimistic bursts.

"Mr Rossberg, I hope that I haven't disturbed you unduly. I was in the neighborhood, and I simply had to

speak to a countryman. Egypt . . . can sometimes be
too . . . Egyptian, if you know what I mean. I miss home.
As you seem to be the closest thing to that, naturally, I
thought of you. I do hope you might feel the same."

With that, the colt plopped herself on the sofa,
slipping her vanity head scarf from her head. Rossie
noted the wedding band now keeping her huge diamond
engagement ring company.

"Please, Anne, call me Rossie. Of course, I am
delighted to see you. I was just having some wine. Care
for a glass?"

Aisha eagerly extended a slender tanned arm for
the glass he offered.

"I love the sunsets here, don't you Rossie?"

"Part of its charm, I suppose. Especially here on
the Nile. Sometimes the water reflects the buildings.
Parallel universes. The one we live in and then the other
one."

At this comment, Aisha began to cry.

"Oh Rossie. You have no idea. Two universes. Yes. I suppose that's why I'm here imposing on your hospitality when I should be at home, preparing for my husband's evening."

"We have more in common than we admit, have we not, my dear?"

Aisha put her feet up on the couch. "One minute you're here breathing in the soft desert air. Hearing the sound of the muezzins calling the faithful to prayer. Did you know, my husband is Catholic?" She didn't wait for an answer. "The next minute, you feel international. Important. Like the Middle East depends on your empathy. On your understanding. Back home, you know, I'm just Anne. A simple girl from Connecticut. But here . . ."

Rossie answered for her. "Here, you are a player. I understand."

Fishing, Rossie inquired, "You say your husband is Catholic. Surely that provides you some separation from it all . . ."

Aisha held out her glass for more. She'd gulped down her first even faster than Rossie. He poured for himself at the same time. He wondered if he dared venture into the tall weeds. Would his friendship threaten her innocence? Would he be her agent of change? Looking at the streaked mascara running down the young woman's cheeks, he knew the answer. Too late. She was already well on her way. All he might offer would be information. Compassion. Understanding.

She shook her head no; there was no separation.

"Yes, well. As you must have guessed, I am Jewish. Not ardently, of course."

"Your Arabic is beautiful."

"Yes, it has been a passion of mine. Also, the fine calligraphy. Hundreds of years have been preserved here. And not just in those mummies over at the museum. Poetry. The culture. Lessons for us all."

The two continued drinking, as each considered their visit. Each wondered how far to take it. Each needed a friend. And that friend, it seemed, was here tonight.

Rossie decided to continue. "I am here, you see . . . I am here to,"

Aisha watched his emotion. She kept quiet as he fumbled for the words. After another long pause . . . " .my wife, you see, was on the cruise ship. Thrown overboard by those terrorists. Because she was a Jew. They saw her Star of David necklace you see."

"My husband's been involved in some shady things."

"He has?"

"Not so heinous, of course. But as a Palestinian . . ."

"Yes, of course."

"He went out on this kayak. He doesn't go boating as a rule."

"I took her to the airport. Paid for an extra bag. She always packs too much."

"Some of his friends, they're older,"

"Her friends survived the attack."

"I think it's over now. Unless there's something else."

"I can't seem to get past it."

"I love him so much." "I will always love her."

The two stopped speaking. The room was filled with their respective feelings. Somewhere in the ether, their emotions met and melded together in a sad mélange leading to more wine.

Eventually, Aisha, nee Anne from Connecticut, roused herself and replaced her head scarf. The slightly tipsy belly dancer made her way down the houseboat ramp, supported by Rossie's fatherly arm. As she turned to go, he took her chin in his hand and delivered a soft kiss to her forehead. He wondered what it would have been like if he and Rachel had had a daughter. That girl would have been so protected . . .

"Take care of yourself, Anne."

Her perfume lingered in his den long after she left. Few people stateside understood the dilemma the two shared. Love of country. Love of a second country. Love of family. And under it all? Righteous indignation at man's inhumanity to man.

Finally, the sun was gone. Rossie was again left alone with his thoughts.

45

"Keep your friends close and your enemies closer." Sun Tzu

The public would be shocked to learn that known terrorists regularly fly the friendly skies. Fouad al Najmi was such an example. Certain security services knew all too well about his past deeds. They watched him more closely than a lion eyes another lion's kill. Under the Company's watchfulness, the international no-fly list posted from Cairo did not include anyone named al Najimi. Passengers saw a blue-eyed Arab with his attractive American wife headed to New York City on vacation.

"Would you care for a cocktail?"

The flight attendant was making her pre-flight rounds of the first- class section of British Airways' Flight 343, non-stop from Cairo to New York. Noticing Aisha's bare head and western style dress, she felt it was safe to offer drinks to the couple.

"My wife is pregnant. But I'll have a glass of champagne. Aisha, dear?"

"Ginger ale will be fine."

Aisha settled into her plush seat and adjusted a lap robe for the trip. She was excited to be taking her new husband back home to Connecticut for Thanksgiving.

"How do you want to do it?"

Fouad's question took her unaware. "Do what, Fou Fou?"

"Tell them. I was thinking maybe we might pick up some sort of grandmother's gift for your mother. Present it at dinner."

Two newlyweds, starting their lives together. Discussing domestic topics. There were no terrorists onboard the plane today.

The flight was long and tiring despite their luxury seats. As the plane passed over the Azores, there was a sudden commotion. A man raced up the aisle, falling over a drink cart. Two men rose quickly and wrestled the man down. The defenders and a pair of handcuffs appeared out of nowhere, and as suddenly as the disturbance began, it was over. Not a terrorist this time. Only a drunk.

Aisha and Fou Fou breathed collective sighs of relief.

"Fou Fou, you know I hate to fly. Now, this! Really, where can one go to escape crazy people?"

"He is Arab. We are watched. You know that. Have you forgotten the frisking they gave us before we boarded? Relax, Aisha. Soon we will be in America. At your parents.' Try to rest now."

Fouad was a man with two lives. The one on a plane, with his beautiful American wife and future child.

And the other one. One not even his best friends could abide. For the time being, he would live both lives simultaneously. There was the meeting with his friend from Dubai that evening. Once again, he would have to lie to Aisha. Go on an errand. He seemed to have quite a few mysterious errands these days.

Aisha was no fool. She knew her man was up to something by the way he scurried around and was increasingly nervous. Also, he talked in his sleep. The incoherent ramblings of a troubled man. She knew more than she let on. Nevertheless, her role, as she understood it, was to stand by her husband in good times and in bad times. When he wanted to talk, he would come to her. Until then, she would continue calmly with her Arabic cooking classes and preparation for the arrival of the baby.

Nine hours later, the al Najimi's landed safely and made their way from Kennedy International Airport into the city. They were staying at Aisha's favorite old hotel, the famous Algonquin, in the theatre district. A welcoming fire was burning in the lobby fireplace as they checked in to their rather small room. Let the tourists go to the other large, slick hotels. Aisha and Fou Fou, experienced New Yorkers, chose an insiders' hotel. The hotel was the famous haunt of the late Dorothy Parker, Robert Benchley, Moss Hart, George S. Kaufman, and the other wits responsible for the antics of the Algonquin Round Table as reported in the New Yorker magazine.

New York City, a month before Christmas, already was decorated and in a celebratory mood. There were women in fur coats and children dressed in fitted wool redingotes. Elegant prams paraded the very young, bundled snugly inside against the cold temperature. Even the dog population sported special holiday attire. Store windows were extravagantly decorated, giving seasonal lie to the myth of world poverty. Horse drawn carriages clip-clopped their way down Fifth Avenue. As if on cue, a soft snow began falling on the scene. The city's picture postcard was complete.

Aisha sat in the lobby parlor as the hotel's resident cat stared her down. 'What are you doing in my home,' he seemed to be asking. Fouad had left on an errand. But Aisha barely noticed. Two transvestite theatre men were ordering drinks at a corner table. Both sported very tall platform shoes, and sparkly gowns. Their makeup was heavily applied and included long false eyelashes. Aisha loved New York, the theatre, theatre people, and the sudden rush of free air she breathed here in this place, her country.

Meanwhile, not far from the hotel, in a nondescript bar, two old friends were meeting.

"Congratulations, Fou Fou, about time you tied the knot! Did you receive my wedding gift?"

"Uh, yes, Geoffrey. But I'm afraid Aisha has been in charge of all that . . ."

"Never mind. I'll just tell you, it was a cappuccino maker. An expensive one, you rat. Actually, Aisha already sent me a lovely thank you note."

"My love."

"And that, Fou Fou, brings me to this. Of course, I am prepared for you. But please think about this. With a child on the way . . ."

Fouad knew his old college friend, a wealthy financier from Dubai meant well. But he had no debt to a grandfather now in his grave. He wasn't with Fouad as the winds drove sand into his teacup. Geoffrey was raised in London. What did he know? 'Take an umbrella with you. It's raining outside.'

"All I can tell you, Geoffrey, is that this is nothing more than an alarm bell I am setting off. No one will be hurt. But many will be frightened."

"Hell, Fou Fou, everyone already is frightened. Where will it all end, my friend?"

Fouad abruptly rose from his chair.

"Sit back down. Please understand. I am your friend. Take it. Take it and do not re-pay me. Unless it is with compassion for others later on. Once whatever this is, is finished."

Geoffrey removed a thick envelope from his jacket and handed it to Fouad. The means to Fouad's ends. Perhaps, a path back to his family's orange grove. The envelope contained a great amount of Saudi money, funds his friend no doubt had skimmed from very wealthy men in his role as their financial advisor. They came to Dubai. Called Geoffrey for a meeting. Ordered up liquor and

women. Gambled. And visited their investments.
Geoffrey was good at what he did for them. But
friendship was worth a bit of larceny now and then.
Around the edges. So long as no one got hurt.

Geoffrey assured his friend, "My friend, I have a
confession to make. These funds are not from me
personally. But my sources are unaware. There is so
much money in the world, my friend, they don't even
miss this. Sahih. Really. I do not lie to you. Don't say
anything further. Our friendship holds. As ever."

"You do not exist. We have not met. You gave me
nothing. "'In-sha Allah,' no one will care in the end,
Geoffrey. Thank you for your discretion. As a matter of
fact, I am the only person involved on my end. No
mouths can speak. There is no one behind the curtain.
Only me."

With these comments, the two men lifted their
glasses, sat back and turned their conversation to more
mundane matters . . . their old days at Princeton, some of
the pranks they used to play, their families. Geoffrey
asked after Aisha, and Aisha's American parents.

"Shu-kran, Geoffrey. They are well. And of course, Aisha is soon to have our first baby. We have learned it will be a daughter."

Laughing, and refilling their glasses, Geoffrey congratulated his good friend. "Ah, Fou Fou, I can just see you now when she grows up and wants to know a boy. You, with a gun at the door. Anyway, a toast: 'To you, Fou Fou, and to Aisha. Long life, health to your daughter.'"

The setting sun on the horizon barely etched the tops of the buildings of Times Square. Many miles distant, at Fouad's vacant Egyptian chalet, a small snake tried unsuccessfully to scale the wall. Eventually, he gave up the task and burrowed back into the warm sands of the Egyptian desert.

46

The Israelis were busy. They had tails on practically everyone . . . Rossie, Melvin, Fouad, Aisha, even Rossie's driver. Around every corner, people were listening. And watching with high powered binoculars and keen eyes. Some of the observers were men. Some others were 'Egyptian women,' wearing camouflage black veils. They kept their eyes on the Russians too, lurking in the shadows.

Not very trusting, these spies!

They watched as the two men arrived separately at the stables located near the historic Semiramis Hotel by the pyramids. One was American, the other, Palestinian. Both men seemed ill at ease as they mounted Arabian horses for a guided tour of the pyramids. Fouad and Melvin were most assuredly not tourists. As in Cyprus, there was a serious reason for their excursion. Israeli binoculars sought to catch details of their ride.

The American, like the Sphinx the group galloped past, never blinked. Nor did he speak to the group of other Americans in the riding party. There was no discernible interaction between the two men. Keen eyes trained in such things, however, noticed that on the trip back the men had switched horses. They knew the excursion was a continuation of the Cyprus meeting. They suspected a trade had just been made in the desert sands. But they had no proof.

God is Great. Grandfather is watching.

The Israelis' surveillance went into high gear. It would not do to lose Fouad or his ill-gotten gain now. The time was approaching for direct action.

As prearranged with Josh, Isaiah took the photograph of Rachel and placed it in a large envelope. He addressed it to Fouad in Garden City.

Poke the terrorist. Draw him from his lair. Frisk him. See what drops out.

47

Aisha didn't open the mail. She left that to Fou Fou. Soon after the couple's return from New York, she noticed the large manila envelope, bearing a Cairo postmark. She carefully placed the mail on the entry table as usual and watched as Fouad sorted through it that evening. He didn't open the envelope. Later, after he went to sleep, she made a quick search of his desk. There was nothing there.

But as Fouad drifted off to sleep, the contents of the envelope were on his mind, haunting his sleep. Someone had sent him a large black and white photograph of Rachel, standing by a ship's railing, smiling. The picture caught black ringlets now touched with gray, and a pair of flashing, intelligent eyes filled with joy as she returned to her beloved Cairo, scene of her youth and indiscretions.

Fouad awoke with a start.

Unfinished business. He had an apology to deliver.

Apology. Such an empty word for terrorist murder-gone-wrong. Sorry. Please excuse our mistake. It won't happen again. You're damned right it won't. Because there was only one Rachel in the world. And now she was gone. With only an apology to a widower yet to be offered up.

Fouad needed to pay his respects, to at least say the words. Who knew what the husband's reaction would be? If it were him, Fouad knew, he'd kill the son of a goat's testicles. He'd exact revenge. Guns are clean and efficient. The final way, perhaps, to drive home the point, to even the field. But not yet.

First, he had some heavy planning to do. He needed to think through every part of his mission. Threatening the State of Israel was large. The world stage demanded nothing less than his best efforts.

The team of professional watchers observed Fouad as he broke a sandal strap outside Groppi's Restaurant in downtown Cairo. He limped awkwardly for two blocks and entered a shoe repair shop. A seemingly innocent errand in the midday sun.

Fouad entered the shop, and walked quickly to the rear of the store, descending a flight of rickety wooden steps.

"Yes, Fou Fou. You have it?"

Fouad greeted the old man wearing a heavy leather work apron in the oppressive heat of his basement office. He handed the man his treasure, a small computer disk that might finally alter the international balance of power. With fingers stained the permanent brown of shoe leathers, the man placed it in his computer and studied its contents.

"Samir, please can you explain what this is?"

"From your American, I presume."

"A fair trade. He needed the cash."

Samir had been a research nuclear physicist for a large country in years past. Mahleshe, never mind which one. There was no one sharper in technical and scientific matters than the old shoe repairman. Suffice it to say, re-soling leather sandals was the least of his skills. Appearances can be deceiving. Everyone has his story.

"I know, I know, my son. Let me have a quick look. Hmm. Pretty complicated algorithms. The Americans have been getting better each year at their encryptions. This might take a while. Can you leave it?"

Fouad nodded. "Of course."

"Give me a week. Khan el Khalili Bazaar. Our usual place. One-week, same time. I'll try to know more by then."

"Shukran, Samir."

"Ca n'a fait rien, Fou Fou."

With that Samir reached for the offending strap, quickly stitching it with his old-fashioned foot-pedaled sewing machine.

"There you go. Good as new."

Fouad left the shop. He was confident his project was in good hands. Samir knew his grandfather years ago. The dependable honesty of family friendship gave him a security bond like no other.

No one would be hurt.

48

For the next week, everyone seemed to stand down. Melvin happily played out his remaining days as Head of Station. When a man has a robust Swiss bank account awaiting him, suddenly his cares melt away. All things seem possible. The sun shines brighter. The future stretches before him. In Melvin's case, a future of fine foods, French wine, and the much-anticipated pleasures of girl-watching on a Parisian street.

An innocent transaction.

No one would be hurt.

Rossie spent his week resting and gathering his thoughts. The professor would be ready for his visitor whenever the hell he showed up. In the meantime, he puttered about the houseboat, fixing a broken window shade here, putting new toner in his printer there. Life's daily-ness provided him a sense of normality bordering on comfort.

His decision to refrain from shooting his son's biological father possibly also played a role in his new-found calmness. There would be a confrontation, no doubt about that. But at least, he would approach the Arab on his own turf and his own terms. The thought of two Mossad agents backing him up to thwart Fouad's future plans added a measure of comfort. Rossie hoped the Israelis would tag Melvin in the process. If they did, he knew, it would be done quietly and beneath the radar of the international clandestine community.

For Fouad as well, the week provided a much-needed hiatus. He could do nothing until Samir delivered his information. Ma'aleesh, may as well enjoy the time. He devoted his energies to Aisha and anticipation of their baby. He worked around the Garden City home. He painted the baby's room. He trimmed some ivy that had overgrown the front gate. He brought his wife fresh flowers from the vendor down the street. He attended to Aisha day and night, reassuring her of his joy that she was in his life.

The two newest arrivals at Funduq Hilton also seemed to be relaxed. After all, there were belly dancers to enjoy, and gin and tonics to drink. While on assignment, they made it a point to try out a different restaurant each evening. Their American accents provided the Israeli agents their cover as people took them for stereotypical 'Ugly Americans.' Lives on hold, as so happens, needn't be spent unpleasantly.

But the men weren't potted plants in the hotel lobby. They were on the move. They entered the shoe shop late at night. A special high-tech device they carried allowed them to locate the computer disc right away. They knew what to do. The disc was inserted in their hand-held computer. Their work didn't take long. The experts went to work. When they were finished, they carefully replaced the disc where they had found it.

Mission accomplished. The Israelis now had their own 'back-door' to one of America's premier weapons systems. A little bit of knowledge is a good thing.

The Hilton Hotel was rapidly filling up.

"The Russians are in town." Isaiah informed Josh.

He was referring to three new arrivals. They spoke Russian and skulked around on their own. They clearly were not happy tourists. Those who saw them, excluding the observant Israeli agents, assumed they were businessmen, in Cairo for commerce. Make a deal and get out. They did not seem the types to spend a day in the Egyptian Museum or tour the ancient pyramids of Saqqara. Business is business. Their serious faces conveyed commerce, and nothing more.

Ma'aleesh. It was a week like no other. The calm before the storm.

On his waterfront, Werner was used to odd requests, and unexpected visitors. Before him stood two overweight Russian men. Their dress was sloppy, and their faces grim. They addressed him in the international French. Lousy accents, he thought with a sneer. Followed by another thought, 'I hate the Russians.' Not tourists. Not businessmen. Men to keep his eyes on.

They waved a stack of Euros at him. With Werner, Euros could override many things. His sneer quickly turned to a welcoming manner. The Old-World charm fairly dripped from his small, fake Euro-Trash body. Of course, whatever they wanted. He was at their complete disposal.

The men were specific. A sixteen-foot felucca with oars and an outboard motor. With a canopy, 'for the desert sun.' Werner closed the deal and immediately called Isaiah.

Very soon, the boat would pass Werner's dock. The Russians would head north to the sea with a new passenger. Mossad's binoculars would make out one Russian steering the craft. Facial recognition research would reveal him as a known K.G.B. agent. The small boat's precise business out there on the Nile would require further checking.

310

49

As the Russians completed their preparations, Fouad made his way to the Khan el Khalili Bazaar as scheduled. His mission was to purchase a new rug for the baby's room. He made his way through the narrow stalls, overhung by colorful materials redolent of the spices and aromas of the Near East and Africa.

While Egypt is an Arab nation, forever linked politically with the rest of the Middle Eastern, it is often overlooked that Egypt is also the eastern anchor of North Africa. This fact of geography provides a certain exotica, not present elsewhere in the Levant. Whirling dervishes dance their hypnotic dances. African chieftains in colorful robes and headdresses roam Cairo's city streets. Distinctly African mixtures of incense mingle with the more traditional Arabian spices such as cardamom, cinnamon, and turmeric. And, of course, thrown in, always there are the few odd Russians, in town on 'business.'

It was into this familiar and teeming mass of human commerce that Fouad entered. He knew his way through the labyrinth of shops, having shopped there many times over the years. The Bazaar's merchants called out their wares, enticing shoppers into their stalls. The cacophony and spectacle alone made a trip to the Khan el Khalili Bazaar worth the trip.

Today, Fouad added another important reason to visit the maize of shops. Payback. A long- overgrown orange grove that no longer existed. Childhood memories fueling indiscreet acts. Samir waited for him with his report. Quietly, Samir handed back Fouad's chip.

His tone was quiet, nearly reverential. "This is a new weapons system, my friend."

Fouad waited. He knew Samir. Slow, plodding, but also brilliant.

Samir continued.

"We can stop now . . ."

Samir was giving Fouad another chance to return to a normal, peaceful life. Back to Anne and the new baby. After a long silence, he continued his analysis.

"A new weapons system like no other. Much better, I would suggest. Clever. With respect, this is only a simple computer program once all the safeguards and bells and whistles are removed. But like no other. Here's how it works. The world's major countries, including Israel, but not Egypt unfortunately, have satellites that constantly are moving in the skies on their appointed trajectories. The satellites serve multiple functions. They stand guard, bring us 100 television channels, and offer the latest in weather news from the upper atmosphere. The devices pass over us at regular intervals and in predetermined travel arcs throughout the year. Yes? Are you with me so far?"

Fouad nodded.

"Now then. Since 1985, satellites have grown increasingly sophisticated. Powerful earth observation instruments have been added each year to aid scientists in

their earth movement predictions. There's GOMOS
(Global Ozone Monitoring by Occultation of Stars,)
there's DORIS (Doppler Orbitography and
Radiopositioning Integrated by Satellite,) and ASAR
(Advanced Synthetic Aperture Radar.) And then, my
friend, there are other acronyms representing tasks that are
less generally made known to the public."

Fouad nodded. "Go on."

"The program provided on this disc will locate
satellites passing over a requested country, logging its
timing and its location with precision. Then on a user's
command, it will disarm the satellite, rendering it useless
to its original operator."

"And so?"

"Oh my. Wait. Just wait. I'll tell you."

Samir stopped to wipe his glasses. Fouad noticed
the left lens, as it had been for years, was still cracked in
the same place.

"Once the satellite is disabled, you then can order it to respond only to your commands, becoming, in effect, your own flying orbital servant. Everyone regards satellites as harmless little orbs moving through space. At their worst, we suspect they can spy on us. At their best, as I have said, they can inform us of the earth's movements and changes – weather, geology, archeology, even the occasional crime scene."

Samir stopped again to light a cigarette. "These can kill too, you know . . ."

Fouad waited again for Samir to finish.

"Of course, all satellites do all of that. But some countries-- the usual suspects, I'm sure -- have added a very special feature to these stations. A few of these satellites are armed with potential weapons systems. But this . . . this . . ."

Samir paused, reflecting on what he was about to say, choosing his words carefully.

"Let me start again. Have you heard about the occasional storms on the face of the sun?"

Fouad. "Solar flares sent to earth. They can interrupt radio communications."

"Potentially much more, depending on the size of the storm. It appears our favorite country has created a new weapon based on that premise. Their satellites must possess unique electrical systems partnered with state-of-the-art delivery systems. The satellites probably are equipped to enable them to harness electrical energy directly from the sun. I have wondered in the past if satellites might utilize sun power one day. Well . . . that day has arrived. Very clever and efficient, if you ask me. Commendable."

Samir paused to pour two cups of tea. It was, after all, nothing more than a friendly visit. The teacups were fine Lenox porcelain. Honey was offered. Another cigarette was lit.

"I think the way they do this is that the satellite rotates periodically to face the sun and then by a process of magnification takes in the sun's rays with a system of high-capacity mirror's onboard the satellite. This allows them to harness the sun's energy for the satellite's special uses. Recent advances in telemetry apparently have allowed them to build this."

Fouad struggled to understand his friend's words. "Solar energy's a good thing – think of it. A new source of energy for the world."

"One would think. One would think. But what if . . . what if the full power of the sun were harnessed and then directed in a single blast at a small country or a metropolitan area? What then, Fou Fou?"

Fouad's eyes widened, finally understanding. "It would interfere with the country's electrical grid."

"Exactly. In the instant you activate, you will be able to send your target back to the Dark Ages. All of their computers, everything electrical will be fried. Virtually un-repairable for decades at best. Congratulations, Fou Fou."

"And no one will be harmed, just the infrastructure of the country . . ."

At this remark, Samir erupted in anger.

"Of course, people will be harmed. Must I draw you a picture?! What you have here are plans related to a weaponized satellite! Hospital patients will lose their oxygen feeds. Operating rooms will go dark. Planes will drop from the skies as air traffic control loses power. How do computers operate? With electricity! No. To the contrary, my friend: Everyone will be hurt . . . either immediately, or in time. Including, my friend, our fellow Arabs in the country. I wonder how carefully you have really thought about this little plan of yours."

The would-be warrior Palestinian, shuddered. Samir was right. Many people would be hurt.

But what of his family? They had lost everything. When would they get their day in court? Who would return their family's farm to them?

With sadness, Samir handed the disc back to his friend.

"Look, Fou Fou. I know. I know what you are trying to do. Of course, we all would love to see this. But you are a Catholic, yes? I am Muslim. Same thing. You have God. I have Allah. But tell me something: How does your soul survive such an act? At what cost to yourself, to Aisha, to that new baby of yours?"

Samir placed a fatherly hand on Fouad's shoulder. As he spoke, he pressed so hard to make his point, Fouad felt pain.

"What satisfaction will there be in the end? I hate to bring this up. But I have to ask you, was Rachel's death not enough for you? Look, don't get me wrong. I am willingly helping you with this. But my best counsel to you, my friend, is to rethink this. It's too large for one man, Fou Fou. Please, I beg you to reconsider. Money? I know this has nothing to do with money. You have enough. Stand down now, Fou Fou. Stand down. Accept the realities of this world."

Fouad tucked his treasure safely inside his shirt and left the shop, Samir's words ringing in his ears. The man who would take back Palestine from the interlopers was having second thoughts. Perhaps his friends were right. Forget the past. Move on. Accept what life has given you. Practice gratitude. Not malice. Never mind the lost land. Move on.

Not unlike the hackneyed global mottos that are flung around so freely -- 'Choose love,' 'Visualize World Peace.' It's simple. Stand down. Forget. Forgive. Take whatever borders you are given. Practice the law. Earn a decent living. Get married. Build your family.

Still more troubling was his last thought: 'Rachel.'

50

An apology for the Devil: It must be remembered that we have only heard one side of the case. God has written all the books.

Samuel Butler

High noon in Cairo.

The hot city streets were dusty like the American Wild West. Desert sirocco winds rattled the houseboat's tin roof. In the midday heat, Rossie dozed off with a good book on his couch. Something woke him.

The wind?

Slowly opening his eyes, he saw a man standing over him, with a pistol aimed at his face. As he focused on the intruder, he thought of Kenneth. His blue eyes staring back at him. The same curious black chip in the iris. What was Kenneth doing . . .

"Sayid Rossberg, my name is . . ."

Rossie felt sick to his stomach.

"I know who you are. Rachel's killer. What now? Have you come here to kill me too?"

Fouad took a step back and silently handed Rossie his gun.

"It's loaded.   So, if you want to shoot me, go ahead. We both know I deserve it."

The two men were locked in an uneasy silence. Rossie, no fool, aimed the gun back at Fouad. It was tempting. He could shove the body right into the river. Only fair after what his men had done to Rachel. He smiled at the thought.

Fouad began again.

"Look, I have thought many times of what I might say to you. There are no words, but I have to tell you that my men made a terrible mistake on that ship. No one was supposed to get hurt. Not that it's any excuse – they took powerful hashish for courage. I have fired them. Not that you probably care about any of that."

Rossie rested his elbow on the couch. The gun was growing heavy, but he had no interest in dropping it. It was satisfying to finally be able to aim a gun at Rachel's killer's head.

"As you may be aware, I knew your fine wife when she was a student in Cairo so many years ago. A wonderful girl. I need for you to know what happened was a horrible, horrible mistake."

Rossie noticed the gold orange filigreed pendant hanging around Fouad's neck.

"Yes, I am aware. Some friendship. So, it was you who returned her necklace to me?"

Fouad nodded. "A sort of message, I suppose. Look, I have nothing more to say. My soul aches for you and your family. I am Catholic. Did you know? Murder in any religion is a sin. Particularly on my own. I am not an Islamic terrorist. Those guys . . ."

"Oh, so now you are saying that you disapprove of terrorism. Sorry pal. Try peddling that story somewhere else. If the truth hurts, deal with it. Do not lie. That only makes things worse. You are evil. At least have the courage to own that."

Fouad was running out of things to say. He was so tense that one of his legs had gone to sleep. He lamely offered what he could: I know you have a son. If you should ever need anything for him – money, or whatever - - . . ."

Rossie interrupted him. "I think we're done here. Please leave."

Fouad turned to go, but Rossie had one more thing on his mind, a token of Isaiah's instruction at Israel's desert-based shooting range.

"Before you leave, al Najimi, I have something for you. Call it a souvenir of our visit."

With those words, Rossie aimed the gun and fired. He wanted the bullet to pass through the swine's heart. But common sense dictated he aim lower. The bullet tore through Fouad's thigh, tearing muscles and bone apart. Rossie could see intense pain register on Fouad's face.

"Inta ibn khanzir aswad. Please don't drip blood on my rug as you leave."

Calling Fouad, the son of a black pig, Rossie could see he had hit his target with the crudity. Good. And so, it was over. Nothing more would bring her back.

Fouad limped out of the houseboat, holding tightly to his leg. It was only right. It was the least he could do for Sayid Rossberg.

Rossie stepped onto his deck and pitched the gun into the Nile River. Probably not the first time a hot gun had been sent to the bottom of that waterway. Nor the last.

On his way inside, he noticed several drops of Fouad's blood on his expensive Persian rug. Blood Rachel had paid for it with her own. Blood that would remain on his rug forever. As a reminder, not of Fouad, but of Rachel and his wonderful son. Still his son, now and forever. Kenneth Rossberg, Jr.

Before Rossie returned to his book, he heard his own voice echo against the houseboat walls: "Never clean this rug."

It was time to leave Cairo for good. But first, he needed to call the Israelis.

51

"An opinion can be argued with; a conviction is best shot."
T.E. Lawrence

Fouad clutched his leg in pain as he staggered up the walkway to the Corniche. He hailed a cab and took himself to the hospital. The doctors were not happy. They needed to operate.

"No. Please. Just clean the wound, nothing more," was Fouad's troubling response.

The doctors assured him the bullet passed through his leg. Infection probably would not be a problem. But the bone was severely damaged. They needed to pin it. For the middle-aged man, the doctors knew crippling arthritis could set in.

There is a Catholic sect, called Opus Dei. They wear stony surplices strapped to their bodies to remind themselves of Christ's pain on the cross. Though a practicing Catholic, Fouad wasn't a member of that extreme sect. Now, he needed Christ on a daily basis. His need was too great to be fulfilled by the tamer rituals of Catholic mass. He needed more. He needed a reminder of Christ's pain to help him bear his own sins.

Also, for what he was about to do.

To the concerned doctors his instruction was clear: "Stitch me up. Pain will not be a problem."

The man's attitude troubled the medical team. But in the end, it was the patient's choice. The doctors wanted to help him. To ease his pain. But no one could relieve Fouad's true pain. It was permanent. Now, however, thanks to Rossberg, he might feel some measure of relief. The sharp physical pain would provide him with a lifelong reminder. Fouad's penance would be his drug of constant pain.

52

The violence of Rachel's death never left Rossie's mind for long. Somehow, however, shooting al Najimi provided him with a measure of solace. While he did not accept the notion of closure, he had to admit revenge brought him closer to achieving it. He slowly turned his attention to his departure. He returned to his writing table and the letter he already had been writing for several months. Occasionally, he paused to gather strength. Before leaving, he knew he needed to complete it. The letter was his final obsession, of a piece with revenge.

Kahlil Gibran's "The Prophet," spoke to him from a printed page:

"Yet I cannot tarry longer . . . For to stay, though the hours burn in the night, is to freeze and crystallize and be bound in a mold.

Fain should I take with me all that is here.
But how shall I?

A voice cannot carry the tongue and the lips that gave it wings. Alone must it seek the ether.

And alone and without his nest shall the eagle fly across the sun."

He struggled over his own words. Some of them came from such a deep and resonant source, Rossie would grow feverish as he wrote. Then he would lift another glass and fall into another troubled sleep. On waking, he repeated the steps. Write. Shake. Drink. Sleep.

53

While Fouad was visiting Rossie and later, the hospital, Aisha returned to the sofa for a brief nap. Now in her fifth month of pregnancy, she craved sleep. She placed a crocheted lap robe over herself and drifted back to sleep. Terrible dream. She could smell a man's foul breath. Who was it? A hand was gripping her shoulder shaking her awake.

"Mrs. Al Najimi. 'Dobree dyen.' Wake up."

As her eyes opened, she saw a large man in a cheap brown suit bent over her. He already was placing duct tape across her mouth. A second man swung her legs off the couch and pulled her to her feet. He roughly tied her hands behind her back. The first man flung a voluminous black burqua over her head. He adjusted the head piece to hide her face.

The men roughly marched her out the front door. She saw with alarm her bwab, her doorman crumpled in a heap on the front portico; the front gate stood open. The men shoved her into an idling taxicab. Aisha recognized their language as Russian. The cab sped out her front drive and made its way to a southern Cairo boat dock. To Werner's rented felucca. For a trip north to Alexandria.

54

Fouad struggled with what he would tell Aisha. She was fighting bouts of morning sickness, and the last thing she needed was her husband limping home with a bullet hole in his leg. What story could he use? Certainly not the truth. That would have to wait a while longer.

Perhaps forever.

The minute he entered his Garden City home through its open gate, he knew a difficult day was about to take a turn for the worse. He lifted his injured doorman and carried him inside growing more frantic by the minute. Where was Aisha? What had gone on here? A large chair was tipped onto its side. The carpet was wrinkled. He had only been gone for a couple of hours.

The doorman's arm and eyes were bleeding. "Sayid al Najimi. Two men. Aisha . . . "

His doorman struggled to tell him what happened. Then he saw the note on an end table. It was written in Arabic.

"Sayid al Najimi. We have your wife. She will be available for pick-up in Sapporo, Japan provided you follow our instructions exactly. A plane ticket is on the couch. Make your way to the Sapporo Park Hotel. Wait there in the lobby. You will be contacted. Bring the disc. You know the one. We will make a trade. The disc for your wife. This can be simple or difficult. It's your choice. You have no leverage. Do not call anyone. Come alone. Don't be stupid."

55

The boat trip took four hours. The heat under the
canopy was intense. The men ordered Aisha to remain
under a wooden seat, out of sight. They spent the trip
speaking in Russian and talking with someone on a
cellphone. Finally, Aisha felt the chop of the
Mediterranean Sea, and a fresh breeze as the little boat
headed out to the open ocean. She motioned to the men.
She was about to be sick. She could see that by now they
were well offshore. The men motioned her to sit up.
Aisha bent over the railing and vomited.

After several hours, they were met by a large ship.
The men guided their charge up a slippery rope ladder.
Once she was safely on deck, she was passed off to three
men who guided her to a waiting female sailor. The
woman shoved her into a ship's restroom. She pointed a
gun at her as she removed her arm restraints. She allowed
Aisha to freshen up and change into a clean pair of jeans

and sweatshirt she provided. Then the woman reattached
Aisha's arm restraints. Aisha noticed a long-sheathed
knife strapped to her escort's thigh as she guided her to a
waiting helicopter.

Aisha tried to get her bearings. As the chopper
took off, dipping and weaving over the waves below, the
woman spoke. Her English was excellent although a soft
palatalization of consonants was a giveaway she was
Russian by birth.

"Mrs. Al Najimi, this is not about you. It isn't
really about your husband either, although he has
something we want. We will land soon in Syria. There,
we will board a military jet that will carry us to a military
airbase in Chitose. Chitose is a military town on Japan's
northern island of Hokkaido. From there, you will be
dressed nicely, as a tourist, and we will make our way to a
hotel in Sapporo."

"And then?"

"Then, we will wait for your husband. If he
follows directions, you may consider this as a rather odd
tour of northern Japan. If not . . ."

The woman patted her gun. Her meaning was clear enough.

56

Fouad grabbed the plane ticket and his car keys. He wrapped a soft kitchen towel around his doorman's bloody head and carefully placed him in the back seat of his car. He drove quickly to the hospital.

"Hashem, I am so sorry. Can you talk? How many were there? When did this happen? Did they say anything?"

It was no use. His doorman was unable to speak. He was bent over the seat. Fouad drove quickly, swerving to avoid carts and pedestrians on Cairo's crowded streets. He pulled up at the emergency entrance to the hospital and motioned for help. Nurses rushed out and took his man from the car.

Fouad yelled at them, "Ma'aleesh. Sorry, I can't stay. Help him! Help him!"

As he put the car into gear again, he made a phone call.

"Mohammed. Listen, I need help urgently. Are you at home now?"

Fouad remembered something his friend showed him several years earlier. It was an item he wanted to carry with him to Japan. The niceties of life suddenly were taking a back seat. A man does what a man must when it comes to protecting his wife and child, especially when he bears responsibility for their peril. His friend was able to help him, and Fouad was in full battle mode as he boarded the plane to Japan with Rome stopover. He was alone in this. No one else could help him now. Only his own wits and strength. Aisha's life and that of his unborn child depended on him.

Fouad raced to the airport, clutching the plane ticket. The disc was taped to his chest. Chalasna. It was over. First Rachel, and now his beloved Aisha. At last, the Palestinian came to his senses. It was time to put to rest his childish dreams. Some things were more important than country. Family trumped everything.

Now he again was paying the price for his actions: putting his family in jeopardy was a stupid decision.

Fouad refused the steward's offer of drinks. He would need a clear head. He and Aisha were in too deep. Once the disc was turned over, common sense told him the Russians would want to eliminate witnesses. Dead people can't talk. These were Fouad's thoughts as the Aeroflot jet lifted off from Rome's international airport.

The last leg of his trip from Tokyo to the northern Japanese island's Sapporo International Airport was only an hour. It seemed like an eternity to Fouad. With his leg throbbing, Fouad spent the long trip deep in worried thought. Samir's words of warning came back to him. His wonderful Aisha and his baby daughter were deeply in danger. His men had finished off Rachel. Would Aisha now pay the price for his actions?

God continued dealing with Fouad as severe turbulence rocked his big plane. The short leg between Honshu and Hokkaido was widely recognized by commercial pilots as one of the worst in the world for rider comfort. Typically, mountain up-drafts and latitudinal ocean currents combine to swing planes violently from side to side, accompanied by abrupt thousand- foot drops. Fouad hoped Aisha's flight had been smoother. On the other hand, was she even in Japan? Was she still alive? Fouad began working a thread on his shirt. Finally, he grabbed it and tore two buttons off before he realized what he was doing. To put himself at risk was one thing. But Aisha too?

The plane finally landed safely. Fouad made his way thirty -five kilometers north by taxi to the Sapporo Park Hotel. There a serene, elegant lobby awaited him. There were a wood-burning fireplace and the requisite giant palms. He searched the Asian faces for his contacts. Nothing. Eventually, he took a seat in a side armchair with a complete view of the floor. He nervously eyed everyone who passed by. No one.

An hour passed. Then two. Finally, a voice close to him whispered, "Sayid al Najimi. Please follow me." A well-dressed Russian man escorted him from the hotel and into a waiting Daishi sedan. The car's Japanese chauffeur wore crisp white gloves. The two men rode in silence. After a half hour, the man turned to address Fouad. "Do you have it?"

"Yes, of course."

"Let me see."

Fouad pulled the disc from his jacket and handed it over. The man quietly placed it in an envelope and then into his breast pocket. The car passed through Otaru on its way to the northern shore. Now they were on a road that was eye-level with the angry grey sea. Spray from the waves landed on the car's windows. The man pulled out a lap-top computer and checked the disc. As they approached the ocean, he addressed Fouad.

"The driver will return you to the hotel. Your wife is on the tenth floor. Here is her room key. Nice doing business with you, Tovarisch al Najimi. Salaamu-alaykum."

It couldn't be that simple. But, as promised, the driver drove him back to the hotel and dropped him off at the front entrance. He entered the lobby alone. It was a trap. He knew that. The key fit the door. Inside, he saw his Aisha. She looked terrified, but she was alive. Two men immediately rushed him from the side. He heard Aisha cry out. Fouad reached out and tripped them.

Adrenaline overcame the pain in his leg as two large men fell on top of him.

As they fell at his feet, the woman who was guarding Aisha lunged at him. But he was ready for her. He aimed an atomizer first at her and then the men, scrambling to their feet. As he sprayed the deadly cyanide canister at the Russians, he yelled at Aisha, "Go to the balcony. Now!"

It was over very quickly. Hashem's loaned spray weapon was deadly and efficient. Soon the three lay on the floor. Their eyes were glazed in the swift death delivered by the lethal gas. He raced to Aisha and untied her. He placed his hand over her mouth and nose as he rushed her from the hotel room. As a final gesture, Fouad placed a "Do Not Disturb" sign on the doorknob.

"Fouad, I don't want to know. Just take me home now. Not Cairo. Connecticut."

"I understand, my love. We will both travel there. Whatever you want. I will tell you everything now. I love you so much. Please believe me."

Their trip from Japan to New York was spent in stony silence. Aisha's carefree view of the world was now over. Her love of a troubled Palestinian, no matter how Westernized, she now saw as a mistake. The only thing holding her together now was the thought of her daughter whom she would be meeting in less than four months.

Fouad tenderly delivered his troubled wife to her parents' home. Then he checked himself back into the Algonquin Hotel in mid-town. He made his way to St. Patrick's Cathedral on Fifth Avenue. And lit a candle. And turned over a new leaf. Again. He knew what God was thinking this time. 'How many chances must the man need?'

And now, Fouad was back at the beginning. It began because of family. And now it had to end because of family. Grandfather would have to step aside for Fouad's new family. The constant pain in Fouad's leg was the least of his troubles. Now, he had a woman to convince. A safe home to create. A new life to embrace. Assuming, of course, that Aisha would choose to take him back. Fouad's phone rang as he sat in a coffee shop on West 57th Street.

"Aisha. Please. I need to talk with you."

But Aisha was determined. It was her turn. Her lecture. Her message to deliver. "Fouad, three people are dead. I was kidnapped and taken to another country. Our child's life was threatened. You need to leave it. Return to Egypt. Alone."

"I am begging you. I can explain everything. I will explain everything."

"Not now. I need time. There are no promises. I am a simple person, Fouad. I cannot take all of this anymore. I am not responsible for what happened in Palestine. And neither are you. You need to get a life. Why don't you go and do that?"

Her last words weren't a question. They were finality. The dead air on Fouad's end was his wife hanging up on him. Perhaps forever. He had waded in too deeply this time. He returned to Garden City on the next flight. When he returned, he called Abdu and Ali. "Please come over tonight. I must speak with you."

When the two friends arrived, they were met by a Fouad they didn't know. He was disheveled and in obvious distress. As usual, they waited to hear his side of the story. Ali spoke first. "What now, Fou Fou? What have you done? Where is Aisha?"

"I must get her back."

"Where is she?"
"Two men, Russians, came here last week while she was napping. They took her, first by felucca, and then by plane, to Japan. They demanded I give them something for her return."

"We don't want to know what that was, do we, Fou Fou?"

Fouad nodded his head. He started to cross the room towards them when his legs gave out from beneath him. He screamed out in agony.

Ali yelled, "Abdu, call a doctor!"

Fouad tried to wave them off before he passed out cold on his carpet.

They delivered him to the same hospital where his doorman still was recuperating. The doctors recognized him from his previous trips. 'This is the whack job who wanted his pain left intact.' It still will require surgery, they warned him. He refused. But as the pain medication weakened him, Ali placed a pen in his friend's hand and guided his signature on the release form. Sometimes close friends step in.

The surgery went well. But serious damage already had been done. His pain would continue, but the infection was dealt with. The medical staff issued him a wooden cane to help take weight off the permanently injured leg.

It's a funny thing about nicknames. They are given in love. Fou Fou was demoted back to Fouad. In the following months, as he talked on the phone to Aisha, or to his friends, no one used his nickname any longer. That privilege, among several others, Fouad would have to earn back.

Only Kahlil Gibran, a poet long dead, understood his dilemma:

'Deep in your longing for the land of your memories and the dwelling-place of your greater desires; and our love would not bind you nor our needs hold you. Yet this we ask ere you leave us, that you speak to us and give us of your truth.'

350

Karen Hagestad Cacy

57

America's new Cairo Head of Station was younger than Melvin. But just as wily. He came to his new posting from four years in Iraq. By any measure, the opportunity to replace Egypt's retiring chief was welcome news indeed. Melvin's office was completely devoid of any personal touches. There were no signs whatsoever that anyone other than a faithful, work-oriented bureaucrat had spent his days here.

Melvin's records were impeccable. Some of the best in the Agency. The man was a legend in his time. A legend if, that is, one valued the monotony of good bureaucrats, moving papers methodically and dutifully. That was their Melvin. They wanted to throw him a going away party. But he was too humble and simple for such a public display of recognition. He seemed embarrassed by all the attention.

Years later, someone said they saw him in Paris, sitting at a sidewalk café, nursing a glass of wine. Paris, where all international scions go to rest. Melvin was a contented man.

At last.

58

" . . . so on and on it will always be . . ."
Cole Porter

Five years later.

Rossie returned to New York. He continued at his university. There were always more aspects to Arab culture that needed to be researched and shared with the world. Of course, there would always be some pieces of knowledge Rossie would leave to gather dust on the shelf, never to be shared with Mid-East aficionados. Nor with his own family. His instinct was not to burden Kenneth with what he had learned from the Israelis. Kenneth was his and Rachel's. He was a good son. He was happy in his skin. Why change all that?

Personal things. Ma'aleesh.   Never mind.

Rossie met a nice woman who was also a scholar in the New York community of intellectuals. She was a bit plump, a woman of a certain age. But Rossie didn't notice any flaws in his new bride. All he knew was that he was no longer lonely. Someone now sat in Rachel's chair, but she was not Rachel. She was another woman with her own personality, but who shared with Rachel her absolute devotion to the slightly bumbling professor. She was someone with whom Rossie could share his life. Together, they attended plays, concerts, lectures – a full range of cultural activities mutually shared. A companion for the rest of time.

A woman to help him forget what had come before.

Life happily centered on family. In the years since he left Cairo, that family grew by another two when Kenneth finally married. Rossie's new daughter in law was an attorney and a politician in Albany. The two had their first child, a baby girl. Her name was Holland. Her eyes bore Kenneth's odd black chip, giving the child an esoteric link back to her Palestinian ancestors. Mother Nature apparently keeps secrets poorly.

It was Rossie's first wedding anniversary on a Sunday. Kenneth insisted on treating them all to a family brunch at the Plaza Hotel's posh Oak Room. There were strawberry blintzes, mimosas, and some nice porridge for the child. And lots of good-hearted laughter.

In the background, an entertainer accompanied the contented scene, playing the piano and singing old Cole Porter songs.

Songs of love and loss.

"I give to you and you give to me true love, true love. So, on and on it will always be. True love. True love."

Rossie happened to glance up as a waiter refilled their glasses. He noticed another family entering the room. The woman looked Middle Eastern. An older American couple trailed behind them. The man was holding a beautiful little girl. She looked to be about five years old. The man was tall with graying hair and striking blue eyes. Close up, Rossie knew there would be a curious fleck of black in the irises.

He walked with a noticeable limp, supported by an elegant jade-handled walking stick.

"For you and I have a guardian angel on high with nothing to do . . ."

As they were seated, he caught Rossie's gaze. In an instant there was recognition. Each man gazed at the other.

Two families.

" . . but to give to you and to give to me love forever true."

On a Sunday in New York.

Enjoying over-priced, but happy family brunches.

As their countries continued to fight, in this setting on this given Sunday, the two nodded a sort of peace. It was in the eyes of each man. There was a resolution, a coming to terms.

Chal'as. It was over.

"For you and I have a guardian angel on high with nothing to do, but to give to you and to give to me love forever true."

358

59

Ismailia several years later.

Finally, the years were kind to Fouad and Aisha. Her silence about what occurred in Japan eventually met his admission of past transgressions. Their love ultimately survived in the form of Isabella, their baby girl. Eventually, the al Najimi's grew to be a typical Manhattan couple. They renovated a loft in the Village to accommodate a growing family. They shopped for fresh vegetables at Zabar's Delicatessen. Aisha purchased hand-embroidered dresses for Isabella at Henry Bendel's. Aisha's parents visited often, pleased with their son-in-law's decision to rejoin his New York law firm.

Eventually, Fouad regained his lost nickname. He accomplished this by turning his back on news of the Middle East. What is a man's life? It is his own, of course. However, once there are children, it is a life to be shared. Fouad became his family's protector and provider of their security. He placed his Palestinian preoccupation on a shelf in the back of the closet. There, a grandson's loyalty rested among cobwebs and other out-of-season items. His warrior days were left behind now. His life now was filled with career, family solidarity, and the pleasures of living sedately.

Aisha and Isabella loved the water. On their infrequent trips to Egypt, they liked to visit Alexandria to play in the Mediterranean. At first, Aisha needed to work hard to push her boat trip to the back of her mind. Chal'as. It was over. Why worry about it now? At last, Fouad sold the Garden City home and desert chalet and replaced them with a beach cabana in Ismailia, where the Suez Canal flows north to the Mediterranean.

On a vacation at the new beach house, the couple lovingly watched Isabella as she dug sand with her new blue bucket. Aisha decided it was time.

"Fou Fou. These past years, I have been keeping something from you, my love."

Fouad poured a glass of wine for Aisha. She shook her head. "We will have another child soon, Fou Fou. I can no longer drink wine, much as I'd love to."

Fouad was overjoyed. His life was overflowing with God's blessings. Only the constant pain in his damaged leg reminded him of his tenuous worthiness for this life. In America, Fouad redirected his energies to helping immigrants and others who truly needed his help. The firm's fat clients eased the way so he could take pro bono cases on the side. It was something. A barter system with the Almighty. With many individuals 'paying it forward,' Fouad concentrated on 'paying it backward.' His past sins were never far from his mind. Amends were made. Good deeds were performed partly in an effort to expunge his past.

And now another child. Proof positive it was finally over. His Aisha would remain with him in spite of it all. Aisha was holding out a large envelope.

"I have something for you. A confession. Years ago, after we returned from our wedding in Cyprus, I was sorting your sock drawer. I found this."

She held out a familiar disc. "I know you have missed it. Since you traded the original one to free me in Japan."

It was her final test for her husband. What would he say, she wondered.

"Aisha, you've had this the whole time?"

"Yes. I had it copied. And this is the copy. Here. Take it now."

As Aisha fixed him with her azure eyes, she had her answer. Fou Fou began to laugh. Then he laughed harder. Finally, he laughed so hard he fell off his lounge chair onto the sandy beach. Aisha and Isabella could not recall ever seeing him in this way. Finally, he took the disc from his dear wife. He walked to the edge of the Canal. And tossed it in.

Chal'as. Finished.

Fouad's grown son and a granddaughter in the United States didn't know he existed. Some family secrets remained intact. But a grandfather resting in the sands of Palestine, his beautiful wife, Isabella and a new baby now claimed Fou Fou's devotion. In the end, it was enough.

As for the truth, one must come to terms with the past if one can. It's a complicated world. Sometimes, all that remains for a man is happiness.

364

Karen Hagestad Cacy

60

Washington, D.C., a few years later.

The guard at the Smithsonian's elegant Freer Gallery of Art stirred to greet a fresh round of visitors to his third -floor collection. That is where the museum's priceless pages of ancient Arabic calligraphy are kept. The guard was now retired. Unable to stay away from his beloved ancient texts and messages for long, he volunteered during weekdays when attendance slowed to only a few.

He never tired of observing the reactions of new visitors to the timeless Islamic artwork. Arabic calligraphy, in flowery and stylized script is the primary means for the preservation of Islam's holy book, the Qur'an. Cultural suspicions of figurative art being idolatrous supported the development of Arabic calligraphy and abstract depictions of holy tenets, dating back to the advent of Islam in 610. Like many of his visitors, the guard had no particular belief in any religion. His fascination with Islamic art was solely secular. Over the years he developed a near devotion to the hypnotic swirls and various styles of writing – Kufic, Naskhi, Maghribi, Andalusi, among others.

The guard's devotion grew to such an extent over the years that he now considered the collection as his own. The venerable Smithsonian Institution only housed the collection for him. He was its true and abiding owner. With a caveat: the guard shared 'ownership' with one other person, one of his 'regulars.'

Today his 'co-owner' was in his usual place on a bench staring at the curvaceous Naskhi pages.   The man spent hours at a time slowly moving through the museum's extensive collection of 9th to 19th century Qur'ans from Iran, the Arab world and Turkey. Unlike the guard, the visitor was a man of faith. Today he wore a yarmulke, the devotional cap worn by proponents of the Jewish faith.

Tomorrow was Rosh Hashanah. And the man would attend his synagogue on L Street Northwest with his wife to commemorate the annual Jewish New Year holiday services. Now seated on the museum bench, he was a nondescript man with a rapt concentration on the art before him. Visitors barely noticed him at all. He was small, and wore thick-lens glasses, giving him a myopic fish-eye appearance as he glanced up. He seemed to be in a sort of meditation as he communed with the ancient artwork.

Visitors naturally had no knowledge of the man's identity. Nor should they. Onlookers had no way of knowing what service he might have performed a few years earlier for them, their children, and quite possibly their children's children. Such is the way in Washington, D.C. Without knowing it, one can rub shoulders with legislators, assassins, diplomats, spies, or simply with individuals of lesser note. Who's to know the difference? People blend in one with another in the nation's surprisingly egalitarian capital. Who would notice a man of a certain age seated quietly on a bench in the Freer Gallery? Who would in their wildest imaginings realize that this particular stranger might have played a part in averting an international disaster in a world that's advanced far past mad?

Rossie was unaware of anyone around him. He

was deep in thought. His meditation was alternately in Arabic and Hebrew. If someone knowledgeable sat near him, he might have been able to make out a mish-mash of ancient Sufi poetry and Hebrew proverbs. The scholar was old and tired now. One could forgive him his odd mix of the world's ancient wisdom.

For him the world's tomes conveying their ancient prophesies were considered as one in their totality. Every religion was of its own consequence. If one were only willing to open his mind and his heart. So few did. Perhaps only the tested are able to receive God's true wisdom.

Tomorrow was Rosh Hashanah. Rossie came to this comforting spot to contemplate his life. In recent years, it had become sedate once again. Yet secrets were still held and still rankled. Old resentments would last. Today the professor, as ever, sought refuge within scholasticism, his eternal refuge. There he communed with the world's great thinkers. There he enjoyed the easy rhythms of desert Sufi poetry. There he felt safe. None of those dead thinkers disturbed his hard-won peace.

At last, he roused himself. He needed to get back to the world of the living. His life. His reality. Never mind what came before. Today's task was long overdue. Life is according to God's will. Today however Rossie would help God in his Work.

His lawyer's office was in Bethesda, Maryland. Rossie caught the Red Line Metro and proceeded to his office. In his breast pocket was a letter. To Kenneth. For later. After he was gone. Not for now.

'*My Dear Son,*' it began. It was the father's intended last act upon his death. To set matters straight. To lay out all of the information about his findings in Egypt and Tel Aviv. The letter took a decade to complete. In it, Rossie expunged the past. His scholarly mind again was unwittingly selfish in its need to tell the truth. The effect truth might have on his son somehow escaped the professor in his desire to set things right.

"The sun! The sun! And all we can become! And the time ripe for running to the moon! In the long fields, I leave my father's eye. And shake the secrets from my deepest bones; My spirit rises with the rising wind."

Rossie had been keeping company with the late Theodore Roethke lately. The poet provided him guidance as he came to terms with how much of the truth to reveal to his son. Family secrets. Everyone has them. But Rossie's were in a class all their own.

The letter went on for more than forty pages. It was handwritten in Rossie's old-fashioned script. The letters were meticulously formed, as though care in penmanship might somehow mitigate the severity of the message. Mahatma Gandhi also took a hand in the letter.

"Nonviolence and truth are inseparable and presuppose one another. There is no god higher than truth."

Harvey Berenson's law office was perched in an office building above the Metro's Bethesda Station. As the Rossberg family's long-standing advisor, he thought he knew all the family's information. Rossie had booked an hour with him to go over a letter he wished added to his Last Will and Testament.

"As you can see, Harvey, it is not yet sealed. I wish for you to read it now. There may be certain legal ramifications to the information, and at some point Kenneth may need your assistance with ."

Words, Rossie's constant ally, suddenly failed him.

" . . with whatever," he concluded lamely.

Harvey's secretary brought in a tray with coffee and tea. Quietly, the friend took the letter and seated himself on his office couch. He pushed his glasses up onto his forehead and began reading. He read all forty pages carefully, taking everything in. When he finished, he retook his seat behind the desk.

Rossie waited for him to speak. Finally, Harvey rose and picked up a fine Chinese ceramic bowl from a side table. He carried it to his desk. He carefully cleared away some books and papers. Then he took Rossie's work and neatly folded it in half. From a desk drawer, he removed a pack of matches. Quickly, and without hesitation, he set the letter afire.

Rossie sat staring at the bowl as the precious pages burned to ash. It was his life, there in that bowl. Finally, the lawyer spoke.

"Now then, my friend . . ."

His glasses slipped down off his forehead.

" . . anything else I can help you with today?"

61

"And You shall cast their sins into the depths of the sea." It was curious that Rossie should begin the Yamim Nora'im, ("Days of Awe,") of Rosh Hashanah with the pedantic act of an attorney, not a rabbi. With the traditional sounding of the shofar, the ram's horn, Rossie heard as never before, its cry for repentance. This year, after Ten Days of Repentance, for the first time in his life, he truly understood the meaning of Yom Kippur, the "Day of Atonement."

His life was spent in the hallowed halls of academia. Now at last, Rossie could see beyond the intellect. No longer was he walking alone. His faith, shelved for so many years, now took over his life. Returning to his Jewish faith, finally Rossie felt peace in sleep, joy in his grandchildren, and forgiveness in his heart.

Ma'aleesh. It is over.

Karen Hagestad Cacy

EPILOGUE

With Russia financing Syria, Iran, and other enemies of Israel, it was time for Israel to bring the Americans in on the joke. Eventually the Israelis 'dropped a dime,' and made their call to Langley with the news. America's weaponized satellites were compromised. It wasn't the first time Israel hacked into America's defenses, nor would it be the last. The difference this time was that they bothered to announce it.

The Americans were grateful for the Israelis' heads up for about fifteen seconds. Then they went to work developing their own anti-solar satellite system. The chess game of diplomacy never missed a beat. The worst mistake of the game is to trust. As President Reagan liked to say, "Trust, but verify."

Mossad assured America that its weaponized satellite system, though in the possession of Mother Russia, was supremely flawed thanks to their prior 'adjustments.' In their storytelling, they also alerted the Americans to a leak in their own ranks. Israel had tricked Russia and blunted Russia's threat to the world community. And now the Americans knew that the

Israelis knew that the Russians knew that the Palestinians knew that certain retrofitted satellites might be on the hunt for more than mere surveillance photographs.

At the end of the day, what they all knew, thanks to Melvin's full retirement program, was that satellites may be programmed using the sun as an ultimate weapon. It was safe to assume that both Russia and Israel would soon follow America and outfit their own satellites with solar flare capture systems.

It was only a question of time. Game on.

Once one knows, soon everyone knows. Some secrets are kept. Others are shared. Secrets pile upon secrets. And then it's on to the next trick. With technology, "Black Ops" is the key to survival. Duplicity continues, as future wars are planned and fought from the comfortable armchairs of today's corporate nation states. As citizens go about their daily lives, sharks circle their evening meal. As ever, it's every man for himself. What's changed in several thousand years of history?

As Melvin packed his bags and purchased a new raincoat for a rainy Paris winter, Josh went back to work in Tel Aviv. As Fouad returned to the practice of law in New York City, Rossie retreated to the comforting walls of academic certainty. The actors assimilated and re-learned their lines. Between plays, everything returns to normal. Whatever normal is.

As for the Palestinians: they continue to stand by watching as battles are fought in their name. As their struggle is cloaked in the homilies of the Bible and the Qur'an. As the world's powers use their plight as a reason to advance their own interests, and their own causes.

Somewhere along the line, the Palestinians have been overlooked. The real people are neither terrorists nor professional whiners. They are readers, thinkers, farmers, family people. People of faith. They are families with children and grandchildren. They are people who, arriving home at night, enjoy the sweet aroma of a wonderful dinner about to be served. They are people who laugh, and who have a joie de vivre.

Some Palestinians stand up. Are angry. Seek solutions in the only way the world seems to understand – through violence. In the end, it has nothing to do with religion. Nor fanaticism. It's the land. The world took their land and refused to return it. At some point, a man of education, a man of the law, a man who believes in the true scales of justice might take matters into his own hands.

Such a man was Fouad al Najimi. Grandson. Father. Friend. Husband.

Son of an orange farmer in Palestine.

Mah'Salaameh.